Storm Singing
and
Other Tangled Tasks

FABLED BEAST CHRONICLES

Storm Singing
and Other Tangled Tasks

LARI DON

 Kelpies

Kelpies is an imprint of Floris Books

First published in 2011 by Floris Books
This new edition published in 2014

The publisher acknowledges subsidy from Creative
Scotland towards the publication of this volume

Cover font designed by Juan Casco
www.juancasco.net

 This book is also available
as an eBook

British Library CIP Data available
ISBN 978-178250-139-8
Printed in Great Britain
by DS Smith Print Solutions, Glasgow

To Mirren, for her honest comments on the difficult things I make my characters do; to Gowan, for suggesting the best selkie name ever; and to Mrs Findlay's P5 class at Inverkip Primary, for their excellent selkie research

Chapter 1

Clip clop clip ... splash!

"Stop giggling!"

"We're not giggling."

"Yes, you are! Walking on seaweed with *hooves* isn't easy, you know."

Helen tried not to laugh as Yann slithered over another wet rock.

"Come on, Rona," she whispered, "let's walk in front of him so we're not watching him slip and slide. He gets *so* grumpy when he's embarrassed."

Clatter ... splash!

"Don't look back," muttered Rona.

"Why not?"

"He's just landed on his rear end in a rockpool!"

Helen couldn't help looking. When she saw Yann

floundering in a deep pool, she took a couple of steps back, grabbed his hand and tried to pull him out.

"Don't be foolish, human child. You can't lift a horse's weight! Back off, so I don't stand on you."

With an inelegant lurch, he jumped out. Water ran down his boy's back and off his chestnut horse's body. He shook his long auburn hair and flicked a tiny crab off his withers.

"Stop staring! Just leave me alone to go at my own pace over this horrible beach."

Yann moved his front left hoof gingerly forward, aiming for a small flat patch of sand, but his back hooves slipped, and he splashed into a shallower pool.

"For goodness sake!" Rona marched off, her smooth hair bouncing against the furry rucksack on her shoulders, her ankle-length dress trailing in the rockpools.

Helen watched Rona walking away, then glanced at Yann, who might break a leg if he went too fast. There weren't any splints long enough for a horse's leg in the first aid kit hanging from Helen's right shoulder. Should she chase after Rona, or follow behind at Yann's pace?

Yann yelled suddenly, "Rona! Come back!"

"No! I can't be late!"

"Come and look at this!"

"Look at what, the seaweed in your tail?"

"Rona Grey, I'm serious. Come here!"

Rona turned back, glancing up at the sun in the same irritated way Helen's mum checked her watch when she had to get Helen to school, Nicola to nursery and already had animals queuing outside her vet's surgery.

"What?" Rona demanded.

"Look at that sand ..." The centaur pointed between his front hooves.

Both girls stared at a clear patch of sand.

"There's nothing there!" they said at the same time.

"Precisely. There's nothing there. It's completely smooth. Something has been rubbed out."

Helen peered closer. The stretch of sand *was* utterly smooth. She looked at other patches of sand between the rocks. They were marked with bird footprints and the soft lines of the last tide.

Rona knelt down and sniffed. "You're right. No windblown grains. No salty crust. Someone has brushed this."

"Someone has covered their traces," insisted Yann. "Someone who doesn't want anyone to know they've been here."

"Who?" asked Rona, her irritation turning to worry.

Yann shrugged. "Someone spying on the Storm Singer competition?"

"But it's a public event. Any sea being or fabled beast is welcome to watch. And humans don't know about it."

"I know about it," said Helen.

"Only because I invited you."

"We can't tell who it is unless we track them," said Yann. "We can't tell what they want unless we ask them." He cracked his knuckles and grinned.

Helen sighed, and Rona shook her head.

"It's a peaceful competition, Yann, not a battle," said Rona. "I'm sure someone brushed the sand for a perfectly sensible reason."

"I'll investigate," announced Yann.

"*You?*" snorted Rona. "*You* are struggling to walk in a

straight line on this beach. I suppose I'd better go." She looked at the sun again.

"You can't go," said Yann. "You only get one chance to enter the Storm Singer competition, Rona, and if you win that, it's your only chance to become Sea Herald. You can't be late. I'll go."

"No," said Helen. "I'll go. You two get to the competition at your own speeds, and I'll check out this possible spy."

"If you find a spy, Helen, what will you do?" demanded Yann. "If you find a kraken or blue man, a sea kelpie or sea serpent, a nuckelavee or giant eel, what will you do?"

Helen frowned at Yann's scary list, then shrugged. "See if they need a plaster? Play them a solo on my fiddle?" She patted the violin case on her back.

"Don't joke, human girl. The edge where sea and land meet may be a holiday destination to you, but like any joining of two worlds, it draws evil beings from both."

Helen grinned. "I've dealt with a power-hungry minotaur and a child-stealing Faery Queen in the last year. I can sneak up on a seaside spy."

Rona wailed, "But if *you* go, Helen, you won't hear me sing!"

"Yes, I will. Your volume and confidence have improved so much in the last two days, I'd hear you even if I was still in Taltomie."

Rona blushed. "Do you think so? If I'm louder and more confident, it's because of your coaching. You're much better at performing than me."

"You write better music, so it evens out. Now get going, and I'll track down your mystery guest. I'll probably be in the audience in time for your songs, and if not, just project loudly enough to reach me wherever I am. Good luck!"

They hugged, and Rona smiled. "I'll get to Geodha Oran faster without you two anyway."

She ran down to the sea's edge, pulled her furry rucksack off, flapped it open, and swung the sealskin cloak over her shoulders. She shimmered in the sunlight reflecting off the sea, crouched on the rocks, then bounced into the water.

A seal.

She waved a fin, and swam off.

Helen turned to Yann. "You carry on along the seaweed, while I go on this wild-goose chase."

"If it's something as small as a wild goose that's been covering its tracks, I'll be delighted. Anyway, I'm coming with you."

"You're as wobbly as a newborn foal on these rocks. What use will you be?"

"The creature isn't on these rocks. The patches of cleared sand lead up the beach, towards that cliff. Even if it isn't doing anything sinister, it seems to be taking an inland route to the venue. So I'll get there faster and safer by following it."

Once Yann had struggled to the base of the cliff, he pointed up the steep rock wall. "A path, with more brush marks. Let's climb up."

Now it was Helen's turn to feel insecure. Yann trotted up the gritty narrow path like a goat, while Helen concentrated on every step.

When they got near the top, Helen whispered, "I'll peek over, I'm smaller and quieter than you."

She edged past Yann and saw an expanse of pale salt-blown grass, with grey rocks scattered along the cliff edge as if they'd been tossed there by storms. "It's clear. Nothing here."

Yann stepped up, and checked the landscape carefully, just in case Helen had missed a sea monster right in front of her. He nodded. "It's clear, and I can't see any tracks on this grass. Let's go towards Geodha Oran. If this creature is watching the contest, we'll spot it on the way."

As they followed the jutting and jagged coastline, Helen asked, "What's a Sea Herald?"

"Pardon?"

"I thought Rona was competing in the selkies' Storm Singer competition, but you said this was her only chance to become a Sea Herald. What did you mean?"

"Hasn't she told you, all those mornings you've spent screeching on the beach?"

Helen shook her head, and Yann smiled down at her, like he always did when he explained something Helen didn't know.

"This afternoon's competition, ignorant human child, is just for selkies competing to become a Storm Singer, the highest level of sea singer. Today's victor then enters a contest between selkies and other sea tribes, to become Sea Herald. Hardly any Storm Singers get the chance to be Sea Herald, because these contests are held very rarely, so Rona is under a lot of pressure to win.

"Her mum and two cousins are Storm Singers. Her great-grandmother was a Sea Herald. Rona has a family reputation to uphold. Maybe that's why she didn't tell you, in case it made you both nervous."

Helen frowned. "She did say it was a family tradition

to win the Storm Singer competition. She's wearing the dress her mum wore when she won. But she didn't say that if she wins she'll have to enter another competition! I don't know if I can coach her through more songs. She gets so *anxious!*"

"You won't have to. The Sea Herald contest isn't a performance, it's a race and a quest. If she becomes a Storm Singer with your help, she'll need my help to become Sea Herald."

"Rona? In a race and a quest? You're kidding!"

Helen wished she hadn't given Rona so much advice on performing. Perhaps Rona would be happier if she didn't win this competition, then she wouldn't have to endure another one.

But Rona's greatest pleasure was to write and sing songs, and the winning Storm Singer was invited to sing at lots of fabled beast gatherings.

Then Helen heard distant voices and faint laughter.

"We're nearly there," said Yann. "Let's find a place we can watch as well as listen."

"What about the ...?"

Suddenly they both saw it.

A rock, on the cliff edge.

A pool of shadow behind the rock.

A shape, shifting, in the shadow.

Helen and Yann stopped.

The figure moved round the rock, peered down at the crowd below, and the bright afternoon sunlight touched its head.

Helen and Yann gasped.

Chapter 2

"What *is* that?" Helen whispered, as they crouched behind a pile of stones.

"I have no idea," said Yann.

Before the figure had slithered back into the shadow, they'd seen it clearly in the sunlight. But instead of shining *onto* the creature, the sunlight had shone *through* it. Helen had seen a crouched body, clear and gooey, with purple lines and pink circles inside transparent flesh, and a huge oval head.

"You don't know what it is?" she asked.

"No."

"I thought centaurs knew *everything*!"

He scowled. "I know all the fabled beasts of the land, but we don't actually study sea beings ..."

"So you don't know any more about sea creatures than I do? You're just as ignorant as I am!"

"Not *quite* as ignorant." His scowl softened into a grin. "Usually I know at least one more thing than you do, which keeps me far enough ahead that you think I know everything."

Helen shook her head. "Rona will know what it is, even if you don't. We can describe it to her later. All we need to know now is whether it's dangerous."

"It doesn't look very hard and scary," muttered Yann. "It looks like someone sneezed it."

"What's it doing here?"

"Maybe it's a fan of seal singing." Yann didn't sound convinced.

Helen peered over the stones. "If we can find a big enough rock on the cliff edge, we'll be able to watch the competition and keep an eye on the spy."

Fifteen minutes later, they were hiding on the far side of a lumpy rock on the very edge of the cliff. Helen knelt down to look at the venue, Geodha Oran, a high narrow inlet slicing inland through the cliffs.

On the lower ledges she saw older selkies in their smooth blotched grey seal form, and higher up she saw young selkies in their human form, with silky tunics and straight hair, nibbling fishsticks and giggling.

She saw Rona, perched in human form on a ledge with five other competitors at the landward end of the inlet, where the rock walls would funnel their voices out to sea.

"Don't wave at her," ordered Yann. "If she waves back, the snot monster will know we're here." He glanced round their rock, towards the spy's hiding place, which was closer to the singers' end of the inlet. "It's not moved. I'm a little concerned that it covered its traces, but I don't see what harm it can do from up here."

"Could it knock the rock down onto the competitors?"

"I've considered that. Look at the rubble round the rock's base. It couldn't be rolled, it would have to be lifted and thrown, and I doubt that lump of mucus has strong enough arms to lift a rock that size."

So they sat, Yann with his legs folded elegantly under him, Helen with her feet dangling over the cliff, taking turns to keek round at the spy and look at the assembly below.

Then Helen noticed two ledges which weren't filled with selkies. One ledge glittered with silver scales and pale wavy hair; the other ledge was a shadowy blue.

"I thought this was a selkie competition. Who are they? Or don't you know?"

"Of course I know! They're observers from the other clans entering the Sea Herald contest."

Helen pointed to the silvery ledge. "Are those ...?"

"Yes. Mermaids."

"And the blue people?"

"Blue men of the Minch. They ..."

But a large selkie, with a deep scar on his face and neck, called for quiet. The Storm Singer competition had begun.

The six competitors lined up on the singing ledge, and the scarred host announced the running order. Rona's name was at the end.

Helen settled back to enjoy the music, and to judge for herself if anyone sang as well as Rona. She listened to the first selkie sing a fishermen's lament in human form, followed by a sea shanty as a seal.

Each competitor would sing three songs: a traditional song, a song they'd composed themselves and an improvised song. The rules also stated that the selkies had to sing at least one song in their seal form, and at least one in their human form.

Helen wasn't impressed by the first seal, Rona's cousin Rory from John O'Groats, sixty miles east along the coast. She hoped to hear melodies which would inspire her to create new fiddle tunes, but his songs were repetitive, and his voice, singing the long vowel sounds selkies love, was reedy.

Helen glanced round at the creature. It was still hidden in the shadow.

The next competitor, a tall selkie from Shetland, sang her first song in human form, so Helen could follow the words. "Another one obsessed with fishermen."

Yann sighed. "These selkie songs are all the same."

"Rona's songs are more original."

Rona respected the old songs, but the ones she wrote herself were influenced by her adventures with her friends, and the music she heard on sleepovers at Helen's.

"If she's too modern," said Yann, "the older selkies won't vote for her."

Helen closed her eyes, enjoying the original rhythm the Shetland selkie had written for her own song, even if it was yet another ballad about a selkie falling in love with the fisherman who'd stolen her skin.

Yann muttered, "Why don't they just whack the human on the head with an oar and grab the skin back? It's like they *want* to be captured and live their life trapped on land."

When the third competitor, from the Isle of Man, started to sing in Selkie, Helen couldn't understand the lyrics, so she leant back to check on the spy. It was almost impossible to see anything in the black shadow, surrounded by the bright sunlight bouncing off the yellow grass. But the creature still seemed to be squatting behind the rock, listening to rather than watching the competition.

She shrugged and turned back to listen to the Manx selkie singing her own composition, a spooky song about sailors trapped in sinking ships. Then the host announced the subject for her improvisation. The selkie trilled a scale to get herself warmed up, and began.

Helen shook her head. "She's copying a Western Isles lullaby. It doesn't really work for a song about eels lurking in caves."

"One less for Rona to worry about," said Yann.

The next competitor was from Rona's own tiny selkie colony. Helen sat up straighter. "That's Roxburgh. I've heard him practise with his dad. He's really good. He could be absolutely brilliant, if his dad would let him do it his own way, instead of bossing him about all the time."

Yann frowned as Roxburgh's voice ripped up the cliff towards them. "Is he better than Rona?"

"Not *better* than Rona, but he sings the traditional songs with a huge amount of emotion. Listen."

"It's like he's torturing the words," said Yann.

"It's crowd pleasing. He's singing it the way they all wish they could."

Roxburgh flung himself into the chorus, sounding as if he was about to burst into tears, or scream in murderous anger, with every single note. Helen sighed, and turned round to check on the creature.

And the sun went behind a cloud.

As the sunlight dimmed, the shadow vanished.

Helen could see a transparent figure. Its purple skeleton. Its pink innards. Its see-through stomach, filled with two partially digested fish.

"Yuck! Look at this."

Yann stretched round, but the sun reappeared and dazzled them both.

As the sharp black shade hid the spy again, Helen saw one more thing.

A bag. A thin fishskin bag, like Rona's mum carried. On the ground at the spy's feet. Wriggling.

"What did you see?" asked Yann.

"It's like a jellyfish squished into a gingerbread-man shape, and it has a bag, filled with something moving, something *alive*."

Helen heard the first few notes of Roxburgh's own composition, a battle hymn about his selkie king ancestors, as she whispered urgently to Yann, "What do we do?"

"We attack it before it attacks the selkies!"

"If it's going to attack them, why didn't it attack at the start? And what's in the bag?"

"Weapons, perhaps, or something it's planning to tip on the selkies' heads. We can't wait until it attacks to find out." Yann pushed up from his kneeling front legs. "I'll grab the bag."

"Don't be silly. You can't creep up on it with hooves. I'll go."

"Don't be daft. You're not ..."

Helen didn't have time for a repeat of the eeny-meeny-miny-mo argument on the beach, and Yann couldn't shout after her without alerting the spy, so she ignored him and slid round the rock on her tummy.

She crawled through the dry grass. If the creature looked round, her red fleece and blue jeans would be easy to see, but it had its back to her and the gentle rustling of her approach was covered by Roxburgh's loud voice.

When she was halfway to the spy's rock, she saw a pale arm move inside the shadow, reaching for the writhing grey bag.

The creature was about to launch its attack!

Chapter 3

Helen had no time to be slow and careful now. She scrambled to her feet, and ran forward at a crouch. Then she heard thudding behind her and a yell of, "*Down!*"

She fell to the ground as huge hooves sliced over her head and smashed onto the earth just in front of her.

Helen leapt up and ran after the centaur. When she reached the rock, Yann was on the far side, tall and solid, arms crossed, blocking the spy's route to the cliff edge.

Helen nodded in approval. Yann wasn't planning to fight this odd beast, just stop it attacking the assembly below. She matched his position on the other side of the boulder, aware of the cliff edge four steps behind her, but standing strong, feet shoulder-width apart, like she was ready to perform onstage.

Helen heard Roxburgh start his improvised song,

about killer whales stalking seals. He sang with less power than normal, as if he was saving his voice, which made no sense because this was his last song.

Helen couldn't see Yann because the rock was between them, but she could see the creature's shimmering back. She heard the centaur's confident voice, pitched low so he didn't disturb the singer below. "Don't move any closer, mucus monster."

The creature swung round to face Helen. Its skinny body was made of see-through jelly, filled with thin purple bones and pink internal organs. Helen recognised the throbbing heart and expanding lungs from her mum's anatomy books. She looked up from the two large fish disintegrating in the creature's stomach, to stare at its lilac face and pale eyes.

Its purple skull was huge, but at least it didn't have any teeth. Though that hadn't helped the fish, which had been swallowed whole.

The creature shambled towards her. Its head didn't seem secure on its neck. None of the bones in its lanky purple skeleton actually connected; they were floating separately in its jellied flesh. And it had lacy frills of pale pink skin at its wrists, neck and ankles.

It was taller than Helen. Almost as tall as Yann. But it was made of blobby jelly, it didn't have teeth or claws, and it was decorated in *pink*. Helen wasn't really scared of it. However, it would be foolish not to take it seriously.

It took a step to the side, trying to get round her.

She blocked it with a long step of her own.

It stepped quickly back to the rock, to get through the gap. But Helen, who'd played this game in the playground when she was her wee sister's age, was already there.

"You're not getting past."

"Yes, I am," whispered the creature wetly.

"No! I won't let you disrupt their competition."

"You will not stand in my way. You cannot resist the power of the sea. The sea will always claim what belongs to the sea." It lingered on every "sssss" sound, hissing its way through the sentences.

It stepped to the side again, a long fast step, swinging the bag on its stringy arm.

This time Helen didn't block it. She grabbed the bag.

She seized handfuls of the scaly material in her fists.

"No!" the creature squealed, trying to pull the bag out of her hands. "Give that back!" Its voice was getting louder. Perhaps it didn't care if the audience below heard. "Let go!"

Helen didn't let go.

"You cannot resist me!"

Helen heard Roxburgh's voice increasing in volume to drown out the creature's shrieks.

"You cannot resist the power of the sea!" The creature tugged hard but Helen tightened her grip.

There was a soft laugh, and Yann appeared, blocking the creature's back. "Neither you nor the sea can resist the strength of a puny human girl! Give up, snot monster, and go home."

As Helen pulled harder, she was horrified to see the creature's arm stretch, getting thinner and paler, but she kept her weight on her back foot and didn't let go, even though the purple arm-bones were getting further and further apart.

She didn't want to pull this creature apart, but neither did she want it to drop a mysteriously wriggling bag on Rona's head, so she kept hauling backwards.

Suddenly the lace around the creature's right wrist uncoiled and flicked out. Long transparent strings whipped across Helen's left hand, then coiled back to the creature's body.

Helen gasped at the burning pain from the red welts rising on her skin. It might be pink and frilly, but this creature could sting.

She stared at the tightly curled tentacles, hoping they wouldn't attack again. Hoping if they did, she'd have the courage to hold on.

"Let go, dust-dry child. Surrender to the power of the sea and give me my bag!" screamed the creature. Roxburgh's voice grew even louder.

Helen was afraid to move back towards the cliff, and afraid to move forward towards those stinging tentacles, but she was determined not to let the creature have the bag, so she dragged her hands suddenly downwards.

The bag ripped open, shreds of fishskin dangling from both their fists, and water gushed over their feet.

The creature's rubbery arm bounced back into shape with a squelching pop. Without a jelly arm to absorb the recoil, Helen fell backwards, landing hard on her backside.

She flung her hands out behind her, and the edge of the cliff slid away under her fingers. She scrabbled forward, almost falling into the writhing mass which had oozed out of the bag.

Helen saw jellyfish, sea urchins, and a heap of other poisonous, stinging or spiny creatures. The bag had been full of the sea's nastiest booby traps. The creature was scooping the living weapons into its four-fingered hands.

Yann cantered behind Helen to block the way to the cliff. Helen crawled away from the twitching pile of poison, and leant against the rock. She could hear Roxburgh still singing below, his voice more powerful and more beautiful than ever, despite the disturbance above.

The creature gathered as many weapons as it could hold, and took a step towards the centaur. Yann spread his arms to block the way. It threw an orange jellyfish, but Yann punched the blob towards the rock, where it stuck for a moment then slithered down into a crack.

Helen saw Yann raise his fist to his mouth to suck the pain from his knuckles and she yelled, over Roxburgh's rousing chorus, "Don't put it in your mouth, it might be poison!" Yann grimaced and shook his hand open instead.

Helen stood up, considering how to distract the creature from behind, though Yann was doing fine on his own. The creature couldn't see past him to aim at the crowd.

The creature stepped closer to Yann, trying to throw over his horse's back. Yann swivelled and kicked out with his front right hoof, which squelched sickeningly deep into the creature's chest. It squealed in pain, and dropped its weapons under Yann's hooves. The centaur made a face as he landed hard on the jelly and spines, mashing them into the earth.

The creature wailed, "No!"

It swung out its arm, not in a fist, but like a whip, and its tentacles flicked at Yann's eyes. The centaur reared up, so the tentacles slashed across his shoulder instead.

But Yann had stepped too close to the edge, and his

unbalanced weight was now all on his two back hooves, one of which was sliding off in a clatter of stones. Helen realised he had only one hoof on solid ground and his weight was pivoting on the cliff edge.

She leapt forward, reached up and grabbed Yann's hand. It felt like she was holding the weight of a race-horse and rider, but she held on tight and leant away from the cliff for the split second it took Yann to regain his balance and bring his front hooves down.

There was a moment of silence, then the crowd below began to cheer and clap.

Yann kept Helen's hand in his fist and grinned at her. "So you *can* lift a horse's weight. Thank you, human child!"

She let go and turned round. "Where is it?"

"It gave up. It ran out of weapons, or ran out of courage."

Helen saw a pink splodge lurching towards the cliff path, and thought she heard hissing laughter over the applause.

Yann stared at the strings of jelly and broken spines under his hooves. "I didn't mean to kill them, but I couldn't avoid them."

The cheering from below faded into quiet, and Helen realised Roxburgh had finished his song.

Yann blew on his stung hand. "I don't think they were cheering for us."

Helen and Yann peered over the cliff together.

A few selkies were brushing dust and gravel from their hair or fur. The rest were pointing fingers or fins up at Helen and Yann. All except Roxburgh, whose fists were held high in triumph, and Rona, whose head was in her hands.

Chapter 4

"Our apologies for disturbing you," Yann called down.

"How dare you interrupt our contest, you impudent half-boy!" the scarred selkie bellowed back. "You and Miss Grey's other dry-shod friend will come down here *now*, and explain yourselves!"

Helen saw a ripple of heads turn towards Rona, who was now staring straight ahead, trying to ignore her friends and the disapproving crowd.

Helen stepped away from the edge, round the pile of spines, tentacles and gloop.

"We should deal with our injuries first." She pointed with her throbbing hand at the red welts on Yann's shoulder.

She swung down the green rucksack containing first aid equipment she'd "borrowed" from her mum's surgery, and pulled out a blue book. She always carried an old vet student book about exotic animals, which was sometimes useful for treating wounded dragons or injured phoenixes, but for this long weekend in Sutherland, she'd borrowed a library book about first aid at sea.

"Jellyfish," she muttered, flicking to the index, then studying the pictures on page 27. "Moon jellyfish? Lion's mane? Man of war? What kind of jellyfish was that, Yann?"

"It wasn't a real jellyfish, Helen. It was talking. It was walking. It had luggage. You're not going to find it in your book."

Helen shrugged. "There's no agreement about the best way to treat jellyfish stings anyway, and we don't have vinegar, lemonade or toothpaste, so we'll just have to make it up."

She checked their hands and Yann's shoulder for any stray bits of tentacle, then searched her rucksack for two white plastic sachets, which she squeezed hard and shook. She threw one to Yann. "Instant cold pack. Hold it to your shoulder, with your sore hand. It might stop any swelling and dull the pain. Perhaps the selkies will suggest a better remedy."

"They're not going to offer us tender loving care, Helen; they're going to give us a row."

Helen swung the rucksack onto her shoulder and adjusted the fiddle on her back, then pressed the cold pack to her aching hand. By the time the next competitor started his first song, Helen and Yann were heading back to the cliff path.

As they felt the cold packs start to work, Helen asked, "How will you get round that slippy beach?"

"Slowly! I'm in no rush to get a bawling out from that big bull seal."

"Don't worry. Once we tell them about that creature trying to attack them, and show them the stings, the ripped bag and the squished weapons, they'll thank us rather than give us a row. Anyway, you're twice the size of any of them. You don't have to worry."

"I'm not worried about us," muttered Yann. "I'm worried about Rona. The audience might think we tried to sabotage her main rival, then they might vote for Roxburgh rather than Rona, however well she sings."

Helen frowned, then winced at a couple of flat notes from the Western Isles selkie. "This one's no competition."

"Will the vote be between Rona and Roxburgh?" Yann asked.

"Probably, so long as no one throws sea urchins at Rona. She might not keep singing like Roxburgh did. He must have really impressed the audience performing right through the fight. He even sang *better* to cover up the noise. I don't know if Rona could do that."

The fifth competitor reached the end of his last song as they reached the top of the cliff path. Helen and Yann stared at the water, shading their eyes against the glare. Helen pointed to an almost transparent pinkish blur, just under the surface, a few metres out in the flat sea. "Is that it? It looks even squidgier underwater. I think it's still listening."

"If it attacks us, we can use those slimy stones as missiles. Come on."

But Helen sat down on the cliff edge. "Let's wait here. Rona's next, and I want to listen properly. I won't be able to concentrate if I'm climbing."

Yann shrugged. "We'll never get to Geodha Oran before the vote anyway, so I suppose it'll do no harm to wait."

Rona started to sing, her high voice soaring over the land and sea.

"This is how seal song should be heard ..." Helen grinned and took off her rucksack, "... at a distance, mingling with wind and waves and seabirds."

The throbbing in her hands was dying down, and she looked up at Yann, still pressing the cold pack to the worst of the stings on his shoulder. The marks on his tanned skin now looked like thin lines from a pen rather than raised wounds from a whip.

Helen relaxed, listening to Rona singing in her human form so she could sing the other two songs as a seal. Rona had decided to sing the same traditional song as Roxburgh, an old ballad about a selkie girl who lost her skin then her heart to a fisherman, in order to show the difference in their styles and voices.

Rona had thought so hard about the meaning of the words, about the loss of skin and sea and family, that even though she didn't sing with Roxburgh's dramatic intensity, her precise voice sliced straight to the heart of the story.

"She is amazing." Helen closed her eyes and listened to every smooth ringing note.

Yann murmured, "Only with your help."

"Nonsense, I just gave her confidence. The talent is all hers."

Rona was tackling a complex run of fast notes, and Helen sat up straight to listen. She didn't realise that she'd put the cold pack down and was fingering the notes on an imaginary fiddle until she heard Yann laugh.

"Music really is your life, isn't it?" he teased.

"Absolutely! Music can tell any story, create any emotion. Music can do anything." They listened as Rona sang loud and strong and beautiful, giving new meaning and intelligence to an old song.

"I thought that was pretty good," said Yann.

"Pretty good? That was the best I've ever heard her sing."

"Better than Roxburgh?"

"Definitely. It was the right decision to sing the same ballad. He was sobbing in his hankie for six verses, but she brought their history to life, thought it through for them, showed them it in a new way. She was perfect."

Yann cocked his head at the sudden silence. "Now she's putting her sealskin on for the song you wrote together."

"I didn't write it with her. That would be cheating. It's her composition. We did work on the performance together though. I had a few ideas to make the rhythm more striking."

Helen wasn't relaxing on the grass any more. She was pacing up and down, as Rona began her song about the selkies' longing to be on land when they were in the sea, and their longing to be in the sea when they were on land, the frustration of being caught between two worlds.

Helen strode along the edge of the cliff, her fingers finding notes in the air. As Rona launched into her soaring chorus, Helen stopped to pull a green hair bobble out of her jeans and tug her dark curly hair into a ponytail, to stop the rising wind blowing it across her face. The only other bobble in her pocket was bright pink, but she handed it to Yann anyway, to tie back his shoulder-length hair.

She stood still, listening to the second verse, watching as the creature below ducked under the waves.

"How's she doing?" asked Yann softly.

"Can't you hear? She's incredible!"

Helen couldn't stop smiling, even when a screeching line of seagulls blew over her head. She didn't like seagulls, but this flock was tossed over the darkening sea so fast she didn't have time to duck.

"She's nailed it!" Helen called to Yann happily. "She's pacing her song to the sea. She's using the pulse of the waves as drumbeats and the breath of the wind as a backing singer."

"Helen, the wind's getting stronger. Come away from the edge." Yann wiped a mist of salt spray from his face, and held his hand out to Helen.

As Rona sang the chorus for a second time, Helen and Yann took a dozen steps inland.

Yann frowned. "If this storm washes away the evidence of the creature's attack, we won't be able to prove what we were doing on the cliff."

The wind whipped round them. A few raindrops hit Helen's scalp, but she didn't put her hood up in case it muffled Rona's song.

Rona's voice picked up in pace and volume and passion, as the waves and wind whirled faster. Helen shook her head in wonder. "Good for her, she's keeping up with the rhythm of the sea and the tone of the weather even when it changes."

"I'm not sure it's happening that way round," said Yann. "Which came first, the storm or the song?"

Battered by the spray thrashing up from the sea, Helen and Yann backed off further, Helen sheltering behind the bulky body of her friend. Yann bent down and yelled to Helen, "Whose idea was it to include the wind and waves in her song?"

"Mine. I thought it would give depth to the music, like singing with an orchestra rather than a solo."

Yann laughed wildly and trotted in a circle round Helen, exposing her to blasts of cold spray.

"You've done it again, bard of the fabled beasts! You've found the magic which all selkies seek! The Storm Singer competition aims to find the few selkies who can call up a storm. Rona is becoming a true Storm Singer, and you told her how!"

Yann grabbed Helen's hands and swung her in a dance, whirling her round the clifftop in time to the calling of the wind, the crashing of the waves, the pounding of the rain and the relentless beautiful singing of their friend.

He lifted her off the ground, Helen gasping and laughing, and Yann shouting, "You came north to turn her into a confident performer, instead you've turned her into a Storm Singer!"

Rona ended her song with a flourish which soaked the pair on the cliff. Yann and Helen slowed their frantic dance, and listened to the audience along the coast cheering wildly. The raindrops had already stopped and the wind was dying down.

Helen noticed the ragged shapes of seagulls being tossed about, far out to sea. "Now I see why Lavender and Catesby didn't come this afternoon."

"Yes," said Yann, breathing hard. "Neither Lavender's

delicate wings nor Catesby's soft fledgling feathers can cope with strong winds. They might have been blown out to sea and never made it back to land."

"Did they know Rona was going to sing up a storm? Did you all know?"

"Of course not. No one has done it for a hundred years! But Lavender was pretty hopeful, and she persuaded Catesby to stay with her just in case."

"Won't they have got battered by the storm at the campsite?" Helen looked anxiously to the east.

"No, the storm was just within the sound of Rona's voice. Come on!" said Yann, still in a hugely good mood. "Let's go down to the venue."

"Wait, I want to hear her last song, and the vote."

"There's no need for a vote! They might ask her to sing again as an encore, but there won't be a vote."

"Why not?" Helen was suddenly worried.

"She has won by right. She is a Storm Singer. No one can deny that. The vote is only to select the best sounding singer when there's no true Storm Singer. Rona has *won*! So we'd better go and give her a hug."

As Rona sang a bouncy improvised song about fish playing tricks to escape seals' teeth, Helen shoved her lukewarm cold pack in the top of the rucksack, and followed Yann carefully down the cliff.

She stopped halfway, and looked at the water below. In the blur of dying swells, she couldn't see any pink or purple. Perhaps the creature had gone. Or perhaps it was still listening, from further out to sea.

Chapter 5

By the time Helen and Yann reached the base of the cliff, seven selkie elders were striding along the beach towards them.

"Cheats! Vandals! Saboteurs!" One of the tall men was jabbing a long finger at them, almost spitting in anger. Helen recognised the hooked nose and blotchy skin of Roxburgh's father, and saw Roxburgh cowering in embarrassment behind him.

"Cheats!" he yelled again, as the group of selkies closed around the calm centaur and the slightly nervous girl.

The shortest selkie there, Rona's mum, glared at Helen and Yann, then turned to Roxburgh's dad. "It was not cheating, Sinclair, because it made no difference to the result. Rona won by acclaim. The noise from above made no difference."

"No difference! Of course it made a difference! But my Roxburgh could have sung up a storm too if he hadn't been distracted. He could have sung up a much greater storm with his power and volume then your mimsy little Rona managed."

"You cannot prove that!"

"*You* cannot disprove it! He was probably just about to sing up a storm when that clumsy clodhopping farm animal kicked those rocks down!"

Helen felt Yann's leg muscles tense beside her. She hoped he had more sense than to start an argument when they were already in trouble.

"Nonsense, Sinclair." Rona's mum kept her voice calm. "Roxburgh was already on verse three of six permitted verses when the shouting started. If he had been going to sing up a storm, waves and wind would have started to build by the second chorus."

Sinclair stepped right up to her, his bare feet gripping the slippery rocks, and snarled at her.

The huge scar-faced selkie barged between them. "Now Sinclair. You know that a true Storm Singer can cope with distractions, even attacks, during a song ..."

"Roxburgh did cope! He sang wonderfully, no matter how noisy these land creatures were!"

"He sang through the disturbance, but he didn't sing up a storm."

"Strathy," Sinclair appealed to the host, "you know my son would have more chance of winning the Sea Herald contest than that little lassie Rona." He shoved his tall gangly son forward.

Strathy shook his head. "We do not choose our Storm Singer for size, speed or strength, but by the power of their song. That policy has given us many successful Sea Herald contestants."

Sinclair opened his mouth to make another objection to Rona's victory, but the host growled, "Stop! Rona won. Roxburgh did not. We are not changing the rules. We are not changing the result. Instead we are asking what these two were doing on the cliff, and deciding what should be done with them."

The semicircle of seal folk turned and looked at Helen and Yann.

Strathy said, "Horse boy. Human girl. Explain your highly insulting behaviour."

Helen and Yann hadn't discussed what they would say, nor who would say it. Yann glanced down at Helen, and she pointed with a tiny gesture back at him. It wasn't wimping out, she told herself, because her ignorance about selkie etiquette could make things worse. Anyway, words were Yann's music.

"Esteemed elders of the seal people," the centaur said, speaking far more formally than he did nowadays with Helen and his other friends, "please do us the honour of accompanying us to the scene of the disturbance. I will explain our undignified behaviour on the way to the clifftop, where I can show you evidence of what we fought there."

Sinclair objected to following a centaur's orders, but Rona's mum was eager, and Strathy and the other elders were curious, so Yann led the selkies in their shimmering grey cloaks up the narrow path. He described what he'd seen on the beach and why they'd gone up the cliff. Helen trailed behind, hoping to avoid telling any of the story herself.

As she reached the top of the path, she heard a voice whisper her name. She whirled round. Rona was just behind her, smiling hugely. "Thank you, Helen! I would never have won without you."

"Yes, you would. You're the best songwriter and best singer I've ever heard."

"I wasn't a Storm Singer until you came. I only sang up a storm because I used the wind and waves as the rhythm of the song. That was your idea."

"I was only trying to improve the song, not magically manipulate the weather. Why didn't you tell me you were hoping to sing up a storm?"

"The clue's in the name of the contest. Storm Singing! I thought you knew."

"Rona, stop assuming I know this fabled beast stuff."

"Even if you didn't know what I was trying to do, you still helped me win, and I will always thank you for that." Rona hugged Helen, her strong swimmer's arms squishing Helen's hands to her side.

"Ow!"

"Sorry. Let me see." Rona looked at the pink welts on Helen's hand. "You need to keep this cool."

"I've already done that. You should have seen them before." Helen frowned at the faded marks. The storm might have washed away the evidence on the cliff, and her first aid was soothing away the evidence on their skins.

"So tell me what did this to you," Rona said, "and why Yann nearly fell off the cliff."

As they walked to the spy's boulder, Helen described the monster and the fight, echoing the more flowery retelling she could hear Yann giving ahead.

When she'd finished, Rona said, "A sea-through!"

"Yes," agreed Helen. "It was nearly transparent, almost see-through."

"No, that's its name. It's called a sea-through. The proper name is cnidaree, but most selkies call them sea-throughs."

"Are they dangerous?"

"Their stings are nasty, and they like to eat selkie pups, but they don't risk it often because it's difficult to hide the evidence with those transparent tummies. They're usually in a bad mood when they're in their landform because they don't like being out of the sea. They're more relaxed in their underwater jellyfish form. In the sea, they're only really dangerous when they band together into blooms, then they get each other all worked up about the sea's rights and belongings.

"Our storytellers say that long ago, sea-through blooms wrapped thousands of tentacles around ships carrying fish, whale oil or sealskins, and pulled them under, and that they sent gangs of sea-throughs ashore to dig up bodies of drowned sailors from graveyards. But no one has seen a bloom for a long time. I'm sure you just met a lone sea-through."

"Why did it try to disrupt Roxburgh's song?"

"Perhaps Sinclair has annoyed the sea-through, and it wanted to stop his son winning? He certainly annoys enough selkies!"

Helen and Rona caught up with the elders just in time to hear Sinclair crowing triumphantly, "There is nothing here. It is all a conspiracy to have the centaur's favourite win!"

Helen looked at the clifftop. It had been scoured clean by the wind and water called up by Rona's song.

Strathy was striding up and down, cloak swirling. "So, centaur colt and human child! Where is the evidence?"

Yann answered confidently, "Do you not recall the evidence of your own ears and eyes? Did you not hear the creature shriek about the power of the sea? Did you not see it trying to throw spines and stings down on you?"

The host shook his head. "We heard no words, just your disruptive yells. We saw no monster, just a clumsy girl fooling about on a cliff and an inconsiderate centaur kicking stones at us.

"You have shown us no evidence of this spy and this fight, so I must conclude that you are lying, that you had another motive for the disturbance." He glanced at Rona. "It does not reflect well on our Sea Herald contestant."

Rona moved closer to her mum, who was biting her lip with small sharp teeth. Roxburgh's dad was bouncing up and down with joy, but Roxburgh was edging away from him.

Strathy looked back at Yann and Helen. "I have no choice but to banish both of you from our precious coastline. You will go inland *now* and you will never come within a mile of the sea again, unless you want the anger of every sea creature raised against you."

"No!" said Rona. "No, Strathy! It *was* a sea-through. Look at their scars!" But Helen's cooling packs had been too effective. The welts on her hands were now pale pink.

Strathy shrugged. "Those marks prove nothing. These land beings could have scraped themselves on rocks."

Yann said smoothly, "Selkie elders are known for their wisdom and justice, so please allow us the chance to put our story fully ..."

Strathy shook his head. "We do not have time

for stories. You have disturbed us enough. Consider yourselves lucky we are merely banishing you. Rona Grey, consider yourself lucky that your natural talent makes it impossible for us to disqualify you."

"But ..." blustered Sinclair, "... but ..."

Rona spoke up again. "We should be thanking my friends, not banishing them. Look ..."

Reaching into the rubble at the base of the rock, Rona dragged out a smaller version of the bag Helen had ripped.

"A fishskin pouch?" said Strathy.

Rona grinned at Helen, and tipped the small bag upside down. Everyone stepped forward to see what fell out ...

Broken shells smashed by birds; a battered but unopened tin of tuna; a cracked mother-of-pearl pendant; a dusty egg-timer filled with sand.

Strathy stirred the pile with his toe. "This is a habit of the cnidaree. Almost their religion. They collect the sea's earth-trapped treasures and return them. I wonder ..."

Suddenly the sceptical elders were looking around the clifftop with new enthusiasm. Within moments Rona's mum found the orange jellyfish which Yann had punched, stuck in a crack in the rock; Strathy found sea urchin spines entangled in heather twenty paces inland; and the oldest elder found a fragment of fishskin clinging to the cliff edge.

The elders went into a quick huddle, excluding Rona's mum and Roxburgh's dad, who was muttering angrily at his son, then Strathy stepped out of the huddle and straight to the cliff edge. Helen and Yann stood close together. Surely they weren't going to be banished from the coast forever?

Strathy raised his immense bull seal's voice. "The selkie elders extend grateful thanks to our dry-shod friends for foiling an intruder's attack on our competition. We shall fête them as honoured guests at our Storm Singer feast tonight, and invite them to be spectators at the start of the Sea Herald contest tomorrow."

The huge cheer from below drowned out Sinclair's peevish complaints and Rona's delighted squeals as she hugged Yann and Helen.

But after the elders headed back to the sea, and Rona's mum left her daughter with strict instructions to be home an hour before the feast, Rona sank onto the ground, put her head in her hands, and started to sniff.

"Oh no," said Yann. "You're not getting all emotional here. You can get weepy on the way back to Taltomie Bay, if you have to."

Yann bent his front legs to let Helen and Rona clamber on his back. He made his usual complaints about being treated like a taxi, but the girls knew he would complain even louder about how long it took them to walk to the campsite on two legs each.

Yann headed inland, cutting off a bulging curve of coast and galloping straight over the moors to Taltomie Bay.

"What's wrong, Rona?" Helen spoke loudly enough for Yann to hear. "You should be delighted about winning the Storm Singer competition. Are you worried about this Sea Herald contest?"

Rona yelled back, "Yes! Very worried!"

"You did brilliantly this afternoon. I'm sure you can win another contest."

"It's not winning or losing I'm worried about," Rona said. "It's living or dying."

Chapter 6

"What?" Helen yelled over the hoofbeats and the wind. Surely she'd misheard Rona's answer.

"It's not losing or winning the contest I'm worried about," Rona repeated. "It's surviving it!"

"What do you mean?"

"The tasks aren't about writing and performing. They're about showing you can survive all the dangers of the sea and the coast."

Yann slowed down, and called, "I can help you prepare for the tasks."

"How can you help, Yann? The tasks happen out at sea."

Yann laughed confidently. "I mean help with psyching yourself up, using your fear to give yourself strength, using your opponents' fear to defeat them. I've won lots of races and fights, so I'm sure I can help you win."

"Stop being so macho, Yann. I don't care about *winning* this! All I want is to be alive at the autumn equinox, applauding the winning Sea Herald, then getting peace to write more songs. I'm delighted to be a Storm Singer, but I've never wanted to be Sea Herald. It's my bad luck that the year I compete for Storm Singer, they need a new Sea Herald too. So I don't want your coaching on the competitive spirit, thanks, Yann. Let's hope I don't need Helen's first aid skills either!"

"But there's no point taking part if you aren't trying to win," yelled Yann. "You could at least *try*!"

"Who are the other contestants?" Helen asked, hoping to stop this becoming an argument.

Rona answered, "Competition winners from two other clans: the mermaids and the blue men."

"Do they have Storm Singer competitions too?" Helen wondered if all the interesting weather round the Scottish coast was sung by fabled beasts.

"No, storm singing is a selkie skill. The mermaids hold a different singing competition, to lure sailors towards them. It doesn't require much talent," Rona sniffed, "just a carrying voice and a pretty face. The blue men pick the blue loon who gathers the most verses."

"*Writes* the most verses?" Helen asked.

"No. Gathers verses. Finds, steals or demands them."

"Why do they ...?"

Yann interrupted, "We're nearly there. You'd better scout ahead to check the campsite is safe."

Rona laughed as the two girls dismounted. "Of course it's safe. It's run by my aunt. It's been safe all week. You take security too seriously."

"It's because my people take security seriously, seal

girl, that no one tells stories about Scotland's herds of centaurs, but every folklore collection has a dozen selkie stories. We stay hidden because we're careful."

Helen and Rona giggled as they walked round the hill towards the campsite, with Yann a careful ten paces behind them.

At home in the Borders, Helen could only meet her friends at night, when they were hidden from human eyes. But the northwest corner of Scotland is the least populated part of Europe, and with a bit of care round the narrow roads and scattered villages, the fabled beasts felt safe there. So she'd really been enjoying this holiday with her friends, roaming the coast of Sutherland in the daytime and actually getting some sleep at night.

Helen's mum wouldn't have let her come north for a long weekend to help Rona prepare for the singing competition if she had known who her daughter's friends really were. Traditional selkies don't have email or phones, but luckily Rona had an aunt who ran a campsite between Bettyhill and Durness. A quick phone conversation with Sheila Mackay to arrange a pickup at Thurso train station had been enough to reassure Helen's mum that this was just a normal long weekend with a normal family.

Just before the girls reached the dip between two of the hills behind the campsite, an airborne blur of orange and purple swerved round the slope.

Rona squealed and ducked. Helen stood still, waiting for the blur to slow down into a peach-coloured bird, and a tiny fairy in a purple dress.

Helen shook her head, still momentarily shocked to see Catesby, this wise sarcastic phoenix, trapped in fluffy fledgling feathers.

Yann trotted up behind them, and said, "Hello, fluffster," then batted away an annoyed attack by his feathered best friend. Meanwhile, Lavender was hovering at Rona's nose. "So did you ...? Were those clouds ...? Have you ...?"

Catesby squeaked at her in his baby bird voice, and the blonde fairy quietened down long enough for Yann and Helen to chorus, "She won!"

Everyone told their stories at once: the spy, the fight, the storm, the Sea Herald contest.

Then, as Helen was about to step round the hill, Catesby squawked and Lavender called out, "Stop! We came to warn you."

"Warn us about what?" Yann demanded. "Not humans? At the campsite?"

Catesby nodded.

Rona said, "Auntie Sheila said we'd have the place to ourselves, because there were no bookings for the whole week!"

Catesby gestured with his left wing for Rona to take a look. Yann hung back, as Helen and Rona crept round the hill towards Taltomie Bay campsite.

They peered over the stone wall, past the two-man tent where Helen and Lavender were sleeping, and the family-sized tent, tall enough for Yann to stand up in and Catesby to fly round. They saw three minibuses with canoes on top and bikes on racks; ten tents of varying sizes and shapes; a whole field of teenagers, and a handful of adults, all in Explorer Scout uniform.

Rona sighed. "All that dry air has driven Auntie Sheila dotty. How can we share a campsite with so many humans?"

They ducked down below the wall, slid back round the hill, and stood up to face an angry Yann.

"Is it as bad as they say?"

"Yes," said Helen. "There are dozens of them and they've got boats and bikes, so they're planning to explore the coast. It might not be safe for you at the campsite, and it's probably not safe for your contest either, Rona."

"Nonsense," said a warm voice behind her.

Helen turned to see a short round woman, with jeans, wellies and long grey hair, walking round the hill. "Nonsense, dear. It'll be fine."

"Why did you let them stay, Auntie Sheila?" asked Rona. "Couldn't you say the campsite was full?"

"Hardly, dear, as there were only two tents pitched when they arrived, and with the contest coming up I knew some humans would be useful ... oh ..." she glanced at Helen, "... em ... isn't it lucky I suggested pitching your tents at the back corner of the field, with the doors facing inland to avoid the wind, because now you can get in and out over the wall without trotting through the camp. You'll be quite safe."

"But how can you say the contest is safe?" Helen persisted.

"Because this unit has stayed here before. They always visit the same islands and climb the same hills. They won't go anywhere near the Sea Herald contest. Not until ..."

Rona jabbed her elbow at her aunt, and Sheila stopped speaking, smiled at them all, then hurried back to the campsite.

"Is that it?" said Yann. "We just hope they don't

notice us in the corner? We just hope they don't go anywhere near the contest? This is ridiculous. All you tinies and human-shaped beasts can stay here if you want, but I'm leaving. If Rona can't be bothered trying to win the contest, there's no point staying anyway." He lifted a hoof and turned to gallop away.

Helen grabbed his wrist. "Don't go off in a horse-sized huff. We *can* stay at the campsite, if we're careful. And even if Rona doesn't want your help to win, she might need your help to stay alive. Don't go, Yann."

He snatched his arm away. "I thought we could have a normal holiday here, but it's not possible. Not for fabled beasts. There are too many humans, and no real wilderness left." But he put his hoof down slowly.

Helen said calmly, "We need to get back to our tents to check we haven't left anything mysterious or magical outside."

Catesby flew upwards to look over the brow of the hill and flew back down, squawking. Yann nodded, as the phoenix flew up again to keep watch.

"They're getting back in the minibuses already, probably going off on a trip," Yann explained. "Once they're away, you lot, at least, can go back to the tents. But first, Rona, if we're going to get you safely through this contest, you have to tell us more about it."

Rona sighed. "The Sea Herald contest is the oldest contest in the world. Older than the Olympic Games or the giants' annual boulder bowling. It's much older than the Storm Singer competition or the other sea tribes' competitions, which were introduced to limit the numbers competing to be Sea Herald."

"Are you competing to be a real herald? To deliver or announce something?" Yann asked.

"Yes, to take a message from one deep sea power to the other, to start a battle."

"A battle!" Yann's voice rose in excitement. "Fantastic!"

"No, it's not fantastic! If the herald doesn't get off the battleground fast enough, the herald gets caught up in the fighting between Merras and Thalas, and can get killed."

"Who are Merras and Thalas?" asked Helen.

"The two great ones whose weights balance the sea. For as long as the sea has been here, the deep sea powers have fought for control of its water, weather and temperature. For many years, they battled every autumn and Thalas prevailed, and for six months it was cold and stormy. Then in the spring, Merras attacked and because she was rested and his strength had waned, she won, so there were six months of warm and calm. And in the autumn Thalas attacked and won, then in spring Merras regained control ...

"So it went on, the rested one winning and the tired one losing every six months, driving the seasons round. But at last, the powers noticed a pattern. No matter how hard they fought, Merras always won at the spring equinox and Thalas always won at the autumn equinox. They were both wounded twice a year, in order for the same thing to happen each time. Eventually, they realised if the winner was inevitable, there was no need to fight. So the equinox battles became rituals, tournaments not wars, where Thalas and Merras flexed their muscles and flourished their weapons, but didn't risk injury or death.

"And tournaments need heralds. If the two sea powers tried to arrange a ritual fight themselves, they would end up fighting about it. So every six months, the Sea Herald takes a formal challenge from the rested power to the ruling power. This week, at the autumn equinox, Thalas will send a message to Merras."

"You have to do it every six months?" Helen asked.

Rona nodded.

"So they pick a new Sea Herald twice a year?"

"No. Once you have the job, you have it until you're too slow or too dead to do it any more. The elders pick a herald young, and hope the herald will do it twice a year for many years. Every single time the herald risks being crushed or drowned as the tournament begins, not because the deep sea powers wish to hurt the herald, but because they wouldn't notice if they did. Even ritual battles between powers larger than islands can destroy smaller creatures.

"The last Sea Herald was a blue man. He retired last spring after sixty years because his ankles were too stiff to sprint any more. Before that my great-grandmother did it for forty-nine years, until she was eaten by a killer whale. But the one before my great-granny was a Cornish mermaid, who never returned from her first Sea Herald trip. So most Sea Heralds last about fifty years, or no time at all."

"What would happen if the herald didn't turn up, or if the message was wrongly delivered?" asked Yann.

"Without the herald to remind them of their agreement to hand over control peacefully after a show of strength, the deep sea powers might fight for real. Then the seas would rise in storms fiercer than any storm since the powers have been at peace, and waves would batter the coast so hard it would change the map forever."

Helen said, "So whoever wins this year's contest takes a message from one huge being to another, to start a ritual battle which could crush the messenger, and if the herald doesn't deliver the message properly, a real battle could destroy the coast?"

"Em ... yes."

"I see why you don't want to win. Why do the sea tribes get involved in this dangerous ritual at all?"

"Because the real battles submerged islands, flooded caves, flattened the seabed, and killed many seafolk and humans. The Sea Herald endangers him or herself, to keep those who live under and by the sea safe. It's a vital job and a great honour. I suppose it's my duty to try to win it."

Rona looked so miserable that Helen gave her a hug. "I'm sure the other competitors are desperate for the honour and would do the job brilliantly. It's not up to you."

Rona took a deep breath. "So, because the herald has to get away from the battleground fast, the first task is a speed trial."

"A race!" said Yann. "Didn't I say I thought there'd be a race, Helen?"

"Actually, you said you *knew* there was a race!"

He grinned. "There's always a race. You'll win a race, won't you?" he said cheerfully to Rona. "Seals are hunters in the water, so you're pretty fast."

Rona shrugged. "Mermaids and blue men hunt underwater too. But yes, a fast seal has a good chance of winning the race."

"Are you a fast seal?" Helen had never seen her friend underwater.

"I'm not sure I'd beat Roxburgh or the other boys who train all the time, but I think I could beat a mermaid and a blue man if I really tried."

"You don't want to win," Lavender objected, "so you won't really try."

Rona sighed again. "If it looks like I'm trying not to win, selkies might be disqualified from future contests. And I don't want to embarrass my family by doing really badly. It might be safe to do well in the race, because there's no danger I'll win the other tasks."

"Why not? What are the other tasks?" asked Helen.

"The third task is a quest to find the herald's holder, the container for the message."

"Excellent!" Yann thumped his fists together. "A quest! We're *great* at quests. We can definitely help with that. You could win that too!"

"I don't want to win it, Yann! I certainly don't want to win *two* tasks because then I'd actually be Sea Herald!"

"What's the second task?" asked Helen.

"It's ... em ... just a challenge to show our control over ... em ... our surroundings ..."

"What do you have to do?"

"Just some singing. A bit like today, sort of ... Oh! That's Catesby's signal; it's safe to go to the tents. Come on." And Rona strode off, at a speed which would win races on land as well as at sea.

Chapter 7

Lavender was lifting tiny dresses off a drying line strung between the two tents, and placing them in a large rucksack on the ground, while Helen and Rona brushed hoofprints off the earth between the wall and the tents.

Catesby was fluttering about, pointing to marks they'd missed. Rona muttered, "Why can't Yann clear up his *own* hoofprints?"

Helen laughed. "Because he'd leave new prints to clear. We need a plan to keep the Scouts away from this corner permanently, so Yann doesn't have to stay on the other side of the hill, and so we don't have to keep clearing up."

Catesby squawked, and Rona dropped her broom. "They're coming back. They must have forgotten something!"

Helen ordered, "Catesby, Lavender, go behind the hill and stay with Yann. Rona, hide the brushes."

"We haven't got rid of all the hoofprints yet!"

"I'll sort the prints." Helen ran to the concrete toilet block, grabbed a hose, turned on the tap and dashed back to the tents.

She soaked the ground, turning centaur hoofprints, bare selkie footprints and phoenix clawmarks into mud.

Helen heard the bus engine growl. "They're nearly here!" She ran back with the squirting hose, wrestling it under her arm as she turned the tap off, then dashed back to the tent. Four Scouts leapt out of a minibus and walked towards them.

"Hi!" said the driver, who was in his twenties, so he was probably a Scout leader. He looked at the muddy ground and Helen's soggy jeans. "Have you had a flood?"

Helen shrugged. "There was a burst drain under our tent, so we're cleaning up." She wafted her hand in front of her nose. "It was the drain from the toilets, so it's quite smelly. You don't want to come too near."

The Scout leader backed away, saying to the three younger Scouts, "You can give them a hand. I'll find those bicycle repair kits."

"I'm Emily," said one of the Scouts, "this is Ben," she pointed to a ginger-haired boy, "that's Liam," she pointed to a boy standing further away, holding his nose.

"You've got *two* tents," Emily said. "One of them is huge. How many of you are there?"

"Five," said Rona.

"Two," said Helen at the same time.

They frowned at each other.

"Two of us," said Helen firmly. "But we've been here for five days. I'm Helen, this is Rona." She held out her muddy hand. The Scouts all shook it, then wiped their hands on their trousers.

"So," said Emily, "do you want help moving to a drier bit of the site?" Helen and Rona shook their heads, and she laughed. "You want to be as far from us as possible? Fair enough!"

Ben said, "I'll put that rucksack back in the tent, before it gets any muddier."

"No! I'll do it!" Helen tried to grab the rucksack before he picked it up. As they politely fought over it, the top layer of packing flew out.

Little dresses, tiny shoes and a spare magic wand.

One pink lacy dress landed on Emily's trainer. She stared at it. "Do you still play with dolls?"

"Yes!" said Rona.

"No!" said Helen.

Helen sighed. How embarrassing was this? "My little sister was coming with us, but she caught a cold and stayed at home, and I forgot to unpack her toys."

Emily shook her head, and the three Scouts walked back to the minibus, discussing whether little kids should be allowed out on their own.

Helen muttered, "I'm not a little kid! I'm nearly twelve." Then she turned to Rona, and raised her eyebrows. "Five of us! Were you going to introduce them to the centaur, the fairy and the phoenix as well?"

"Sorry! I'm not used to talking to real humans."

Helen laughed. "Don't worry, I wasn't any better. Anyway, if they think we're strange *and* camped over a burst sewage pipe, they'll stay away." She shook her head as they watched the minibus drive off again. "Your Aunt Sheila is a bit naïve if she thinks fabled beasts can live this close to humans."

"Auntie Sheila knows what she's doing. She's run this campsite for thirty years, and no human has guessed what she is. She's the only selkie we know who stayed on land after her husband gave her back her skin, even after he died and her children left home. She's pretty good at making your world her own, even though she's a selkie elder."

Helen looked at her watch. "You'd better get ready for your victory feast. We'll join you once it's dark enough to row over without being seen."

Once Rona slipped down to the shore and swam off to join her family on Eilan nan MacCodrum, the island in Taltomie Bay, Helen unpacked Lavender's washing. As she laid the tiny dresses on the groundsheet to dry, she noticed the faint lines on the back of her hand. Helen ran her fingers over the marks. They were tender and itchy.

In the chaos of the Scouts' arrival, she'd forgotten the fight on the clifftop. Now she wondered why the sea-through had attacked the Storm Singer competition, and why it had waited until Roxburgh was singing.

As she considered these puzzles, Helen got her fiddle out. There wasn't room to swing a bow arm in her own tent, so she moved to Yann's taller tent, to play the most intriguing tunes the selkies had sung that afternoon.

When the light outside faded, and she'd played the new melodies into her memory, she returned to her own tent to tidy up Lavender's wardrobe. As she was matching pairs of shoes, she heard a scratching noise outside. She unzipped the door, and Catesby divebombed in, then told Helen something vitally important.

Which she didn't understand.

Helen never understood anything important Catesby said.

She'd known the phoenix for months: first in his elegant, metallic, almost adult plumage; then after he burnt up and re-hatched, growing into these fluffy juvenile feathers. But his squeaky baby bird voice wasn't why she couldn't understand him. She just couldn't understand phoenix language.

All her fabled beast friends understood him, though they had to answer in their own languages. "All you have to do is *listen*," Lavender would say in exasperation. Helen tried, but she couldn't hear any words in Catesby's squeaks and squawks.

Catesby clicked and whistled, then shrieked with frustration.

Helen groaned. "I know you're annoyed I can't understand you! I'm getting *that* message. But I'm still not getting the original message. Sorry. Please do the wing thing again."

Catesby used his left wing to gesture to the door, then towards the other tent.

"You want me to go to your tent?"

He nodded.

"Are the others there?"

He nodded again.

Helen tutted. "Why didn't you say so?"

He squawked in irritation. She grinned, stroking his fluffy feathers, then carried him on her wrist into the bigger tent.

"I have to get changed first, obviously." Lavender was perched on Yann's shoulder, tugging a tiny comb through his dark red hair. "Once we're all respectable, we can head off."

Helen looked at her jeans and t-shirt. "I was going like this. We're going in a boat, to a cave. Anything fancier would be overdressing, wouldn't it?"

"Please make an effort," Lavender said. "It's Rona's celebration."

"I'll brush my hair, and I might put on jewellery, but I can't do anything about these marks on my hand."

Lavender bounced over to look at the fading scars. "Those still look nasty. What was that sea creature trying to do? Will it disrupt the next contest too?"

Helen shrugged. "If it's some enemy of Sinclair's, only interested in stopping Roxburgh winning, then it won't care about the Sea Herald contest."

There was a gentle tap on the outside layer of the tent and Sheila's voice whispered, "I can get the boat ready in ten minutes, if that's ok?"

"Ten minutes!" shrieked Lavender. "But I'm not changed!"

While everyone else got ready, Helen brushed her hair and put on an old coral necklace she'd found in a charity shop. Then they jumped, clambered or fluttered over the wall, and went around the outside of the campsite to join Sheila at the lantern-lit jetty.

Helen looked at the campsite's rowing boat, then at the centaur beside her. "Are you sure about this, Yann?"

"I've flown on a dragon. I can stand in a boat."

"But can the boat take your weight?"

Sheila laughed. "I'm sure it can. It's carried fat

fishermen and all their kit, so it will cope with a few kids."

"Kids with hooves?" Helen muttered.

Sheila crouched down, and picked up the rope tying the boat to the jetty. "If you row from the bow, Helen, and Yann stands carefully over the middle and stern benches, then the boat will be quite low in the water, but well enough balanced. It's a new boat, light, fast and easy to row, so I'm sure you can cope. And I'm not coming with you, so that's one less person to fit in the boat."

"Why aren't you coming?" asked Lavender. "Don't you want to cheer for Rona? Or don't you have the right clothes for a feast?" She glanced at Sheila's jeans.

"I'll cheer from this side. I don't cross the water any more."

"Why not?" Helen asked.

"Most selkies are never satisfied with where and who they are," Sheila said quietly. "We long for the sea when we're on the land, and long for the land when we're at sea. So I've made my choice. I stay on land. I'm happier that way."

Yann took a deep breath, and stepped into the boat, which rocked wildly from side to side. He leapt back onto the jetty.

Catesby squawked. Yann glared at him. "Humans can do it. I can do it."

So he watched the boat, judged its gentle movement on the slight swell, and timed his step carefully. This time he got two hooves in the boat before it lurched and he reversed again fast.

Helen said, trying to sound serious, "In the olden

days, horses and cattle were tied to the back of boats, and they swam along behind. We could try that."

"I am not *cattle*!" Yann said angrily, as he tried again.

Lavender and Catesby didn't manage to hide their sniggers, as it took three more attempts before the centaur finally stood awkwardly in the rocking boat.

Helen stepped lightly into the front of the boat to pick up the oars, checking they were secure in their rowlocks, and once Sheila had untied the rope, Helen started to row. She gasped as she pulled on the oars. She'd rowed her mum and little sister round St Mary's Loch in the Borders last summer, but rowing a boat with a centaur in it would be harder work.

Sheila called from the jetty, as Helen got into a slow steady rhythm, "Will you be alright, Helen?"

"I'm fine. But Yann's not getting any pudding if he wants me to row him back!"

Because she was rowing, Helen was facing the stern, the back of the boat. So she was looking at where they had been rather than where they were going, though she could hardly see the lights of the campsite past Yann's huge bulk. "You're just too *heavy*!"

"Nonsense. The water is supporting my weight, all you're doing is moving us along. If you can pull me up a cliff, human girl, you can row me over the water."

When Helen took a break, she twisted round to see the dark island ahead of them, outlined against the black sky. Eilan nan MacCodrum was like a tipped-over slice of cake on the water: high cliffs at one end, sloping down to a beach at the other.

Helen started rowing again, wishing that her friend Sapphire was here to fly them all from shore to island.

But the dragon couldn't leave her Borders home until she had shed her old skin, so Helen would have to get used to being a taxi service this weekend.

"Stop splashing me, Helen!" said Lavender, perched on the side of the boat. "You're getting my dress wet!"

"I'm rowing as smoothly as I can."

"Stop it!" Lavender squealed again. "Who's doing that?"

Then a voice called:

"We will stop the splash in time,
When you top our verse in rhyme."

Helen stopped rowing. All the fabled beasts looked frantically around, Yann's movements making the boat wobble.

The voice had come from the sea.

Chapter 8

Lavender lit the air above the boat with shaky lightballs from the end of her wand.

The boat was surrounded by a ring of people, bobbing in the sea. Their wet heads and upper bodies were dark and shiny in the magical light.

"Finish our rhymes, or we soak you!" said the nearest boy in a cheerful voice.

They all swam forward and grasped the edge of the boat, one at the bow, one at the stern, and four on each side, rocking it slightly. Then they chanted:

"A human, a horse, a firebird, a fairy,
A strange group to be crossing the seas."

There was a pause.

"Finish the verse, or we'll soak you," repeated the smiling boy, hanging on beside the port-side rowlock to Helen's right.

"Finish the verse, or we'll *sink* you!" said the boy at the bow, behind Helen. They all chanted again:

"A human, a horse, a firebird, a fairy,
A strange group to be crossing the seas."
Yann's deep voice continued:

"This mixed magic boatload might make you wary,
But we're friends, so let us past, please."

"Perfect!" said the boy to Helen's right. "Now we need three more verses for the other three in the boat."

Helen whispered to Yann, "Who are they? What should we do?"

Yann replied, clearly and openly, "Helen, meet the blue loons, the sons of the blue men of the Minch. This tribe have a nasty habit of drowning people who can't create poetry up to their low standards of doggerel, but don't worry. I can make up rhymes for most words except orange and silver."

"But a poetic pony isn't enough," called a boy near the stern. "You *all* have to answer or we won't let you past. Can the lilac blossom rhyme?

"The bright green sea doesn't need flowers,
No petals of pink, purple or red."

Lavender answered in her high voice:

*"I'll be gone in a couple of hours,
Fast asleep in my dry flower bed."*

The smiling boy said, "Rhyming *and* punning! Well done!" But they didn't stop their uncomfortable rocking of the boat.

"Your turn now, ugly ducking," said another blue loon, on the starboard side.

Helen gasped. How could Catesby complete a rhyme, when he didn't speak English?

*"It won't be easy, but to save your friends,
You must rhyme, even though you can't talk."*

After a tense pause, Catesby fluttered above their heads, and chittered a chant with the same rhythm as the blue loons' couplet, which ended in a loud squawk.

The blue loons laughed. Helen hadn't understood Catesby's verse, but that squawk at the end had definitely rhymed with "talk".

Helen had no time to feel relieved, because Catesby's success meant she was next. The boy to her right called out:

*"So human child, you can't get past,
Till you tell us the end of this verse."*

Helen looked up at Yann. He shrugged. He was powerless here, away from the land where he was so fast and strong.

The blue loon repeated the lines:

"So human child, you can't get past,
Till you tell us the end of this verse."

Helen had no ideas at all. The rhythm was simple enough, but she had never liked writing words for tunes. Violinists weren't expected to sing.

The voice behind Helen called angrily, "Rhyme *now,* human child, or we'll sink the boat. Once you're in the water, we'll sink you too, unless you give us the rhymes in your head."

"I don't have any rhymes in my head," she said quietly.

And the blue loons attacked the boat. In one sudden shocking movement, the ones to port dragged the boat's edge down, the ones to starboard shoved upwards, and the boat lurched to the side.

Helen screamed as she slid out towards the water. She let go of the oars and grabbed the side of the boat. She wedged her feet under the bench in front. She flung herself sideways to starboard as if her weight could count against the force of ten teenagers determined to drown her.

Yann roared and Helen felt the boat jerk as the centaur leapt into the air then crashed down again to stay in the boat.

Then the boat swung back, and righted itself. The blue loons had only tipped it once. It wasn't an attempt to drown them. Just a warning of what would happen if she didn't answer.

Yann was shifting his hooves to get his balance, Catesby was fluttering in the air above her head, and Helen groped about for the oars, vaguely aware she'd lost something even more vital.

"LAVENDER! Where's Lavender?"

A tiny cough came from her right.

Lavender was clinging to the port side of the boat. She was completely soaked. "I'm going to a party!" she yelled furiously. "And I look ridiculous!"

"You won't get to the party unless the human girl rhymes," said one of the blue loons.

"We won't get to the party unless I find both oars," muttered Helen. The left oar was in its rowlock, but the right oar had slipped free.

She peered past the blue loons at the water. The oar should float, but it might already be out of reach. "More light, Lavender," she whispered, "I've lost an oar."

Before Lavender could shake the water off her wand, Helen saw the oar. The blue loon nearest her was grinning as he pushed it back through the rowlock.

As she bent closer to grasp the oar, he murmured, "Don't overthink the rhyme, just listen to the rhythm, then answer it. It's easy, you have it in your head already."

Then he called out, "Last chance, human child, rhyme the third time of asking, or we overturn the boat.

"So human child, you can't get past,
Till you tell us the end of this verse."

Helen closed her eyes, mouthed the words along with him, and rather than planning an answer, she let her thumb keep the beat on the oar, and her mouth keep the words going ...

"Thanks for leaving my poem till last,
Because my rhymes are even worse."

"No," the boy at the bow said. "That's not true. They aren't any worse than rhyming seas and please, or talk and squawk. So your verse is a lie and you have to rhyme again."

"You challenged us to top your rhymes, not speak the truth," Yann objected. "We're late for the feast, so let us past."

"A human is most likely to know the answers we need," said a higher voice. "So she rhymes again."

"That's not how we do it," said the blue loon by Helen's right oar. "They've all rhymed, they're free to go."

"Just because you gather at least one verse a day, Tangaroa, doesn't mean you can deny the rest of us our chance," muttered the boy at the bow. "This girl might know our way home."

"Not when we keep changing the rules. They have rhymed. They have the right to pass." He spoke with clear authority, and the others let go of the boat when he did.

He nodded to Helen. "Row on, human child. We'll see you at the feast."

The blue loons swam off, through the black water, towards the dark island.

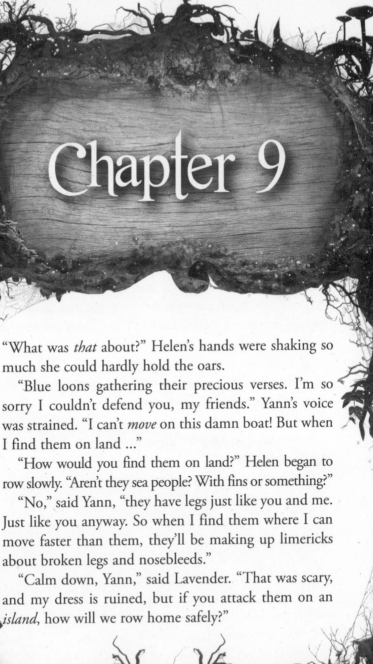

Chapter 9

"What was *that* about?" Helen's hands were shaking so much she could hardly hold the oars.

"Blue loons gathering their precious verses. I'm so sorry I couldn't defend you, my friends." Yann's voice was strained. "I can't *move* on this damn boat! But when I find them on land ..."

"How would you find them on land?" Helen began to row slowly. "Aren't they sea people? With fins or something?"

"No," said Yann, "they have legs just like you and me. Just like you anyway. So when I find them where I can move faster than them, they'll be making up limericks about broken legs and nosebleeds."

"Calm down, Yann," said Lavender. "That was scary, and my dress is ruined, but if you attack them on an *island*, how will we row home safely?"

Catesby squawked his agreement.

"There was not *no harm done*!" snapped Yann. "I was humiliated, Helen was bullied, Lavender was nearly drowned, and they called you an ugly duckling. I can't ignore that. I have my reputation to uphold!"

Helen tried to distract Yann from his plans for revenge. "Why did they want us to make up poetry for them?"

"Too thick-headed to do it themselves," muttered Yann.

"We can ask them at the feast. Politely," said Lavender.

"I'm not asking them for anything except an apology."

"Be sensible, Yann. If you make a battle out of it, they might make it dangerous for us to travel along the coast to support Rona. If you treat it like a game, just boys fooling around, there will be, as Catesby says, no harm done."

Helen remembered the voices threatening to drown them. She didn't think it had been a game.

She followed Yann's bad-tempered directions round the cliffs until they were on the seaward side of the island, invisible from the mainland.

"Where do we moor the boat?" she panted, her arms and back now really tired.

"We don't," grunted Yann. "We row in."

"Row? Into a cave?"

"Yes, and if the tide is already too high after those blue buffoons delayed us, I'll have to duck as you row in."

"Why are we rowing in? Isn't it dry inside? Don't seals need dry land to have their pups ...?"

Yann interrupted her. "Sheila said to take a sharp right at this rock, then we should see the cave."

69

Helen waggled the oars about, trying to make a tight turn, looking behind her at every stroke. She'd only ever steered a boat in open water, and wasn't sure she could navigate through small spaces.

Lavender squealed, "You're splashing me again! You're as bad as those uncouth loons!"

Helen didn't pay any attention to Lavender's complaints, because once she was round the rock, she could see a warm glowing arch in the cliff, suggesting hot food and somewhere to rest her tired arms. She pulled the oars with more enthusiasm.

"Slow down!" called Yann. "We have to go carefully. Sheila says it's not easy with the tide rising, but humans have steered boats into this cave before. It's been the seals' nursery and feasting hall for centuries, except for a few years when smugglers hid their cargo there."

Helen rowed cautiously, with Yann calling, "Left, left more, right now."

Suddenly they were under the low stone arch, and Yann rocked the boat as he ducked down. Helen twisted round to see the width of the arch, and realised the boat would fit through but the oars wouldn't. So she gave one strong pull to propel the boat as far as possible, then hauled the oars in, letting the boat float slowly through.

The boat drifted to a halt in a large cave, with a pool of water at the entrance and dry land at the back, rising up and flattening out to a stone floor, where tables were set for a feast.

Half a dozen selkies dived in to push the boat to a rusty mooring ring, and help the friends out. As Helen lifted Lavender, whose wings were still too wet to fly, onto her shoulder, she saw three other arched entrances round the cave and a large fireplace at the back. She also caught a glimpse of Rona, in a silver dress, sitting at the top table surrounded by selkie elders, adult mermaids and blue men.

Strathy strode up. "Welcome to our feast, honoured guests. You have arrived as we conduct tribal business, so we must ask you to wait with the other contestants and their supporters in a side cave. Roxburgh, would you show the way?"

Roxburgh led them to an archway at the right of the feasting hall. He stood back and frowned at Yann, Helen, Lavender and Catesby as they walked and flew past him, then left them to follow a long sloping tunnel down to a smaller cave, with a deeper pool and a wetter raised floor. The selkies' other guests were already there, sitting on rock stools and benches.

Helen gasped at the sight of the nearest guests, dressed in floaty fabric like the selkies wore, but much less of it. Slimmer and taller than the plump cold-water selkies. Perfectly groomed, with long curly blonde or red hair and beautiful faces.

And fishtails.

The fishtails shouldn't really be a surprise. Helen had read mermaid books as a wee girl. She'd even had a mermaid costume, with a tight shiny blue fishtail which made it impossible to walk properly.

These mermaids weren't walking about either. They were perched prettily on the edge of the pool, giggling and nibbling snacks.

Then Helen saw something more surprising than the fishtails. Almost a third of the posing beauties at the water's edge had shoulder-length rather than waist-length hair, and the fins on their tails were less lacy.

They were boys, with fine thin faces, but strong swimmers' arms. Mermen as well as mermaids.

Helen was used to standing open-mouthed in surprise at the sights of her friends' world. But Yann was standing beside her, also gazing at the mermaids. "I didn't ... I never ..."

The slimmest mermaid, with long red hair, called in a voice as bright as morning and as clear as ice, "Oh LOOK! Our land-based saviours. We are SO grateful for your BRAVE defence of us this afternoon. Please DO join us. We'd LOVE to hear ALL about your adventures."

Catesby snorted through his beak.

Helen nodded. "Absolutely. I completely agree."

Yann recovered from his trance. "Did you understand what Catesby said?"

"No," said Helen, "but we're the only ones not gazing at the mermaids like they're made of chocolate, so I guessed."

Because Lavender was gazing too. "The cut of those dresses. How clever ..."

Helen sighed, and turned to put her rucksack on a rock chair. She noticed the other young guests waiting in the small cave while the elders had their meeting: the blue loons, sitting at a round table. After seeing the mermen, it wasn't a surprise to see that almost half of the blue teenagers were girls. They did have blue skin, blue jeans, grey vests and slicked-back black hair, but they were definitely girls.

Yann noticed them too, and stamped over. Helen followed more quietly.

The blue loons all stood up, and formed a dark line facing the angry centaur.

"How dare you attack the selkies' guests like that?" Yann demanded.

Before the blue loons answered, Helen heard some delighted "ooohs" from the mermaids behind her.

Then the boy who'd rescued her oar stepped forward and held out his hand to Yann. "I am Tangaroa. I'm the blue men's representative in tomorrow's contest. I'm delighted to meet you, land warrior, and I apologise for our dramatic encounter earlier. It is our custom. I'm sure your people also have customs which surprise visitors to your world."

"You apologise?" Yann was surprised to get what he wanted. So surprised, Helen suspected he would demand something else.

"Of course. I regret it if we frightened you, centaur."

Helen almost laughed, as Yann spluttered, "You didn't *frighten* me!"

The boy shrugged his wide shoulders. "We did catch you at a disadvantage. Even so, you all rhymed wonderfully."

Helen put her hand on Yann's flank, while Catesby whispered in his ear, both signalling the same thing: calm down, shake his hand, make peace. But Yann took another aggressive stride forward. Tangaroa didn't retreat, he just kept his hand out.

So Helen stepped in front of Yann, and took the hand. It felt a bit greasy, but she shook it firmly. "We accept your apology, even though you didn't apologise in rhyme."

Tangaroa grinned. "Would you like to join us?" He waved towards the stone table and stools.

Yann said stiffly, "I can't join you until your attack on my person and honour has been avenged."

"If you resent us challenging you in our sport of rhyming, on our element of water," said Tangaroa, "why don't you challenge us to a land sport?"

Yann took a step back, and looked at the blue loons. As if he was measuring them, Helen thought, to see how far he could kick them.

Yann said, "We can't race on this island, as the only decent stretch of grass is on the slope visible from land. And I didn't bring my bow for an archery competition." He glanced at the piles of ropes and chains at the back of the cave. "What about tug-of-war on the eastern beach?"

Tangaroa frowned. "You're challenging us to ten individual tugs-of-war? We'll be late for the feast."

"No," said Yann. "Just one tug-of-war. Me against all of you at once."

The blue loons laughed. Suddenly there was a babble of technical discussion about lengths of rope, who should referee (Catesby volunteered), and how Yann would get to the beach (Tangaroa offered to row him), then they rushed out of the cave, leaving Helen on her own by the blue loons' table.

Not completely on her own. Lavender was still on her shoulder, muttering, "Boys, and their games."

"Better than fighting," said Helen, stretching her stiff arms. "And they weren't all boys."

"Could we go and sit with the mermaids?" whispered Lavender.

"If you want," Helen replied. "I'd just as happily lie down, though, I'm quite tired."

"I'd love to. I've never met a mermaid before."

Helen walked down to the mermaids, who were smiling and waving, almost cooing encouragement.

Helen had experienced the forest faeries' glamour, so she wasn't entirely convinced by the mermaids' perfect beauty. They were wearing so much jewellery and make-up, it was hard to focus on their faces. When she stared, almost rudely, their faces seemed long and pointy with narrow noses and sharp chins.

They kept smiling, and chorusing: "DO join us. DO let us make you welcome until the selkies can say thank you properly."

Helen found herself on a long stone bench, with one mermaid massaging her aching shoulders, another pressing a warm mug into her hands, and another offering a tray of tiny pink snacks.

The mermaid with the bright red hair was perched in front of Helen, her silver tail coiled around a rock stool. "DO tell us about that nasty sea-through. That must have been SO exciting. Or were you scared, or were you confused, or was it all a BLUR? DO tell ..."

Helen told a shortened version of the tale they'd told the selkie elders, and finished by asking, "Why do you think it attacked Roxburgh, rather than anyone else?"

"Oooh," said the fire-haired mermaid, "it could have been ANY ONE of us. You saved us all. We're SO grateful."

That wasn't a particularly useful answer, but Helen could discuss the sea-through properly with Rona later. However, the mermaids might tell her what Rona hadn't wanted to.

"Which of you is competing tomorrow?" she asked casually. "And what are the three tasks?"

The mermaid in front of her answered proudly, "I am Serena, and I have the PRIVILEGE of being the mermaids' representative, so I will be racing and questing and taking part in various challenging ... challenges. But let's talk about YOU! What lovely DARK hair ..."

Helen looked round. Where was Lavender?

The fairy's wings must be drying out, because she had fluttered over to a blonde mermaid, to admire a string of black pearls.

Helen yawned. She couldn't help it. She had climbed up a cliff twice that day, fought a see-through sea monster, and rowed a horse across the sea.

"Sorry ..." she turned back to Serena. "Sorry, what were you saying?"

"Your hair. We know how DIFFICULT it is keeping hair TIDY, with the wind and the salt, so can WE comb it for you?"

"Of course, but I don't need it all fancy like yours."

"This isn't FANCY," said Serena, pulling a comb from a bag at her waist. "You should see us when we get DRESSED UP!"

So Helen sat on the bench, surrounded by mermaids combing her hair and singing. In the damp warmth, with the tickly feeling she always got at the back of her neck when someone else was doing her hair, with soothing mermaid song in her ears, and her tired arms finally relaxing, Helen closed her eyes.

She didn't open her eyes again until she felt cold water touch her face.

She was lying on the bench on her left side. The water was touching her left cheek, her left hip, her left ankle.

It was the sea, rising in the cave.

Helen sat up, and was jerked back by a searing pain in her head. She tried to sit up again, but she fell back down onto the bench.

She was still half asleep, but the chilly water woke her up fast enough to work out several important things all at once:

She was tied down.

By her hair.

To the bench.

The sea was rising fast.

And she was alone in the cave.

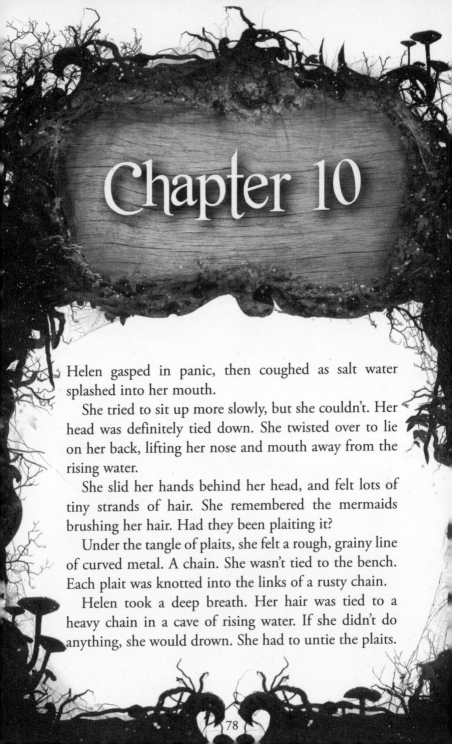

Chapter 10

Helen gasped in panic, then coughed as salt water splashed into her mouth.

She tried to sit up more slowly, but she couldn't. Her head was definitely tied down. She twisted over to lie on her back, lifting her nose and mouth away from the rising water.

She slid her hands behind her head, and felt lots of tiny strands of hair. She remembered the mermaids brushing her hair. Had they been plaiting it?

Under the tangle of plaits, she felt a rough, grainy line of curved metal. A chain. She wasn't tied to the bench. Each plait was knotted into the links of a rusty chain.

Helen took a deep breath. Her hair was tied to a heavy chain in a cave of rising water. If she didn't do anything, she would drown. She had to untie the plaits.

She tried to grasp a plait between thumbs and fingers to unknot it. But her fingers were cold in the water, she couldn't see what she was doing, she couldn't untangle one plait from all the rest, let alone untie the end from the metal. All she did was scrape her knuckles on the rusty chain.

The water was covering Helen's throat now, her face just an island in the water, her elbows and knees rising up either side and in front of her. How much longer did she have before the seawater covered her mouth and nose? How many more breaths could she take?

She concentrated on not panicking. There was time to think her way out of this.

If she wasn't tied to a piece of furniture, just to a chain, all she had to do was lift the chain. Pull it up, and sit up. Then she could walk to the dry part of the cave, dragging the chain with her, and untangle her hair there.

So she grasped the links between her hands and tried to sit up, not pulling with her head, but lifting the weight with her arms.

It didn't hurt as much, but the chain was stretched tight under her, and her arms were at an awkward angle, so she couldn't move it at all.

She was struggling to breathe now, because her attempts to sit up were disturbing the water and pushing ripples up her nose. She had to get out of here. Could she just rip her hair out of the chain?

So she jerked again, hauling her head up, using her tummy muscles and neck muscles, pushing with her hands on the bench. She tugged and pulled, hoping that her hair would break at the ends, or even rip out of her scalp.

It hurt. It hurt worse than anything she'd ever felt. But it didn't free her from the chain.

Helen sobbed as she tried again. Perhaps it would take more strength than she had, to rip thousands of hairs out of her scalp all at once.

She yelled out, "*One more time!*" and pulled again. Her voice echoed round the cave, but her head didn't lift more than a centimetre out of the water.

As she splashed back down, holding her breath so the waves didn't overwhelm her, she heard her voice echo, and wondered whether anyone else had heard it. There was a long tunnel between her and the feasting hall. If she screamed, would anyone at the feast hear her? Would anyone get here before she drowned?

It was all she had left. Once the water settled and her face was in clear air, she took a deep breath ...

Then she heard the most wonderful sound in the world, better than any music: the sound of hooves on stone.

It was the beat she knew so well. The staccato trot of an impatient centaur.

She yelled, "*Yann!*"

"Come on, Helen, you're missing the ..."

Helen twisted round to look at the entrance, turning her face into the rising water, and saw blurs of colour through the salt in her eyes.

Purple. Orange. Silver. Brown.

Lavender. Catesby. Rona. Yann.

All yelling at once: "Helen!" "What are you ...?" "How ...?"

"Shut up and *help me*! My hair's tied to a chain. I'm about to drown!"

Lavender and Rona dashed towards her, Yann and Catesby turned and sped away up the tunnel. Rona dived into the pool and swam round to Helen's right. Lavender hovered above her.

Helen could feel Rona's fingers behind her head, then the selkie surfaced beside her. "There are *dozens* of plaits. I can't untie them all. Back in a minute." She dived off again.

Where had Rona gone? Would a minute be too long? Helen was tilting her chin up simply to breathe.

"Maybe she's gone to block the water's entrance into the cave," said Lavender in a wobbly voice. "Or something else useful. Don't panic."

"I'm not panicking." Helen hoped that was true.

"Keep still, and I'll try an unwinding spell. It's for wool, but it might work on human hair." Lavender perched on Helen's forehead, picking up strands of her fringe and murmuring soft syllables.

Now Helen couldn't see any of her friends. She knew they were all trying to help her. But she couldn't *see* them. She needed someone to hold her hand. Or talk to her. Not mutter on her forehead with little stilettos digging into her skin.

Lavender bounced back in view. "I can't do it! I'm having to release each hair individually and there isn't enough time ... I'm sure someone's coming. Hold your breath. Don't breathe in!"

Helen couldn't breathe in. She was now completely underwater. Her nose, her mouth, her eyes. All under the cold salt water.

There was a splash beside her. Rona stuck her hands under Helen's shoulder, and yelled, "*Lift the chain!*"

81

"I can't, I've tried!" Helen bubbled with the last of her breath.

"I've unhooked it! It'll be easier to move now. Lift, Helen, *lift*!"

Helen put her hands behind her, wrapped her fingers round an oval link and lifted. She felt Rona take the strain too. They both hauled at the rusty chain.

Suddenly Helen was sitting on the bench, water up to her ribs, and a painfully heavy chain draped over her shoulder.

At that moment, Yann galloped in with an axe, and Catesby swooped in with a dagger.

"Too late, boys!" spluttered Helen. "Rona has already rescued me."

Yann splashed into the water, lifted the chain and carried it to the highest point of the cave, Helen following awkwardly, her head still attached.

"I think those mermaids tried to drown me," Helen coughed, as she sat down slowly.

"First things first," said Lavender. "Let's get this chain off you."

"I can cut her hair free," said Yann, waving the axe.

"*No!*" said Rona, Lavender and Helen all at once.

"I'll try to untangle each plait with magic and my fingers," said Lavender, "and if I can't, we'll use Catesby's dagger to slice them *carefully* right at the end, so we don't cut too much off."

Helen lay down on her side, and Lavender started to loosen the plaits one at a time.

"Who tried to drown you?" asked Yann.

"The mermaids. They brushed my hair when you went out for your tug-of-war ..."

"Which I won, in case you were wondering."

"I wasn't wondering, I was drowning. They brushed my hair, and sang to me, and I was so tired after rowing some great lump across the bay that I fell asleep, and everyone went away and left me."

Lavender broke off her spell. "You looked so peaceful, and the selkies called us through for the speeches. We were coming to get you in time for the starters."

"Did you leave me tied to a chain?"

"Of course not! We left you safe on the bench, with no chain in sight. You did have these plaits, though. Your hair will be nice and crinkly when I'm done. The hair you have left anyway."

"So, either the mermaids came back during the speeches, found a chain and tied me to it, or someone else did. But who, and why? And what is this chain anyway?" Helen thumped it with her fist.

"It was left here by smugglers," explained Rona. "A couple of hundred years ago, smugglers hid brandy and tobacco in these caves, and we had to have our pups on open beaches in the autumn. Then one of our chief's daughters started flirting with a Custom and Excise officer's son, and told him about the cave, so the smugglers were arrested and we got our home back. The officers took the boxes and barrels, but the chains and ropes were left behind. That chain was still attached to the wall, which was why you couldn't sit up until I unhooked it."

"So did the mermaids plait my hair so they could tie me to that chain?"

"Serena and her friends just like doing hair," said Lavender, breaking out of her spells again. "I'm sure they didn't plan to hurt you."

"Whoever tied you to the chain couldn't plan it in advance," Yann pointed out, "because no one could know you would fall asleep here."

"The mermaids sang me to sleep," Helen said stubbornly, "so they could come back and drown me."

"Why would they do that?" asked Rona.

"Why would anyone do it?" said Helen. "And why did the sea-through attack Roxburgh? There are more questions than answers today. Are you finished, Lavender?"

"Nearly. The last dozen are all really knotted. We'll have to use the dagger."

"No! You are not cutting my hair with a dagger! Rona, there are scissors in the outside pocket of my rucksack. They'll be too big for Lavender, so could you cut my hair free?"

"You have cutting tools in your bag?" Lavender squeaked. "Why didn't you tell me when I was standing there, watching you drown?"

Helen sighed. "I didn't think. I must have been panicking a little bit after all."

Helen spent an uncomfortable five minutes listening to snipping sounds behind her. She didn't care that much about her hair, not like Lavender did, certainly not like the mermaids did. But having chunks of hair cut out, just before a feast with Rona's family and picture-perfect mermaids, made her feel like a toddler with chewing gum stuck in her hair.

"Ouch! Careful!"

"Sorry!" Rona said. "That's the last of it."

Helen sat up straight. "Am I bald?"

"No!" they all said, too fast to be reassuring.

"Your mane is a bit bushy," added Yann, "and an interesting shape, but it's fine."

"Bushy! And interesting!" Helen wailed. She turned round to look at the chain. Little knots of wet dark hair were tied to four huge rusty links. Rona had cut as close to the chain as possible, and the knots of hair looked like a line of spiders perched on the metal.

Helen lifted her hands to her head. Her hair was damp and crinkly, and her scalp was very tender, but she still had lots of hair.

"Do you want a mirror?" asked Rona.

"No," said Helen firmly. She put her hand in her jeans pocket, pulled out a wet hair bobble, tied her hair into a messy ponytail, and stood up. "It's only hair. I wasn't competing with the mermaids anyway. Thank you all for saving me. Let's get to your feast."

Helen led the way up the winding tunnel, and soon she could hear voices chattering, cups clinking and the occasional burst of laughter.

Were the mermaids laughing right now, imagining Helen cold under the water?

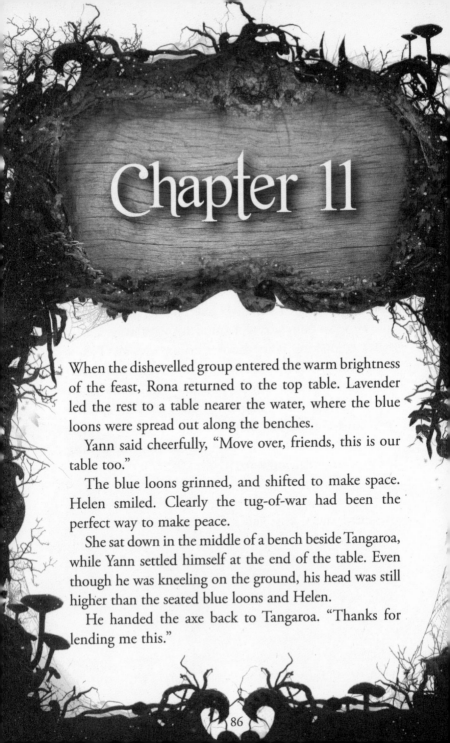

Chapter 11

When the dishevelled group entered the warm brightness of the feast, Rona returned to the top table. Lavender led the rest to a table nearer the water, where the blue loons were spread out along the benches.

Yann said cheerfully, "Move over, friends, this is our table too."

The blue loons grinned, and shifted to make space. Helen smiled. Clearly the tug-of-war had been the perfect way to make peace.

She sat down in the middle of a bench beside Tangaroa, while Yann settled himself at the end of the table. Even though he was kneeling on the ground, his head was still higher than the seated blue loons and Helen.

He handed the axe back to Tangaroa. "Thanks for lending me this."

"No problem, land warrior. Why did you need it in such a hurry?"

"To cut our human friend free from an underwater grave, but I'm glad we didn't need it."

Tangaroa turned to Helen, but before he could say anything, she asked, "Why did you bring an axe to a feast?"

"We always have a few blades with us. Some boats are sturdier than others, and harder to sink. Putting a hole under the waterline usually works."

He hefted the axe through the air before laying it at his feet, then asked, "Was your hoofed friend serious? Were you trapped underwater?"

"Yes. Those murderous mermaids over there tied me to a heavy weight and left me to drown." Helen spoke quite loudly. All the blue loons heard her, and a few selkies turned to look at her.

Then the guests swivelled round to stare at a carved wooden tabletop floating in the water in the lower half of the cave. A table surrounded by mermaids, swishing their lacy tails, flicking their hair over their shoulders, and feeding each other small seaweed snacks.

The mermaids completely ignored their audience, so the guests stared at Helen again. She turned bright red, as she realised she had no real evidence the mermaids *had* tried to hurt her. Lavender said she'd been fine when the mermaids left, and surely someone would have noticed if the mermaids had sneaked away from that floating table. Why would the mermaids try to drown her? Why would *anyone* try to drown her?

Strathy made a loud, provocative remark at the top table, so the guests swung away from Helen to look at him. All except the mermaids, who now glanced at Helen, their pretty faces sharp with surprise.

As the food was served, Helen realised she couldn't reach the mermaids to ask them questions, and they couldn't reach her to drown her or do her hair. So she might as well eat her tea.

She looked at the platters in front of her, filled with fried and dried fish, smoked and steamed fish. Then she looked at the hands either side of her, serving sand-eel stew, stirring fish-egg soup, breaking open baked crabs.

Blue hands.

But sitting so near, looking so closely, Helen noticed the hands weren't blue at all. They were brown. The deep blue came from lines of tightly packed tattoos.

Helen turned to the girl on her right and stared at her upper arm and shoulder. She was decorated with blue swirls and spirals, on top of warm brown skin. The girl wasn't completely covered in tattoos; Helen could see clear patches of skin on the inside of her arm.

The girl saw Helen looking, smiled shyly and said, "Do you want some smoked ray wings?"

Helen spluttered, "No thanks," and turned away, embarrassed at being caught staring. Now she was facing Tangaroa, who was grinning at her embarrassment.

He leant closer and held his arm out for her to examine. But Helen kept looking at his face. The blue on his lips, which made his teeth so white, was the only solid blue on his face. The rest of his face was covered in thin confident lines, arching over his eyebrows, slashing across his cheeks.

Intricate mazes of ink were tattooed onto his arms and shoulders too. Unlike the girl, he had almost no spaces, apart from the palms of his wide hands.

"I'm not completely covered yet," he said, "but I've collected all I need to become our Sea Herald contestant, so I might not bother getting any more."

"What have you collected?" Helen leant forward, examining the back of his hand, and realised the tattoos were made of tiny letters. Tiny words. Long lines of rhyming verse. "Did you write these?"

"We don't write them, we gather them. We demand rhymes from those who put themselves in our hands by coming into our waters."

"You've threatened to sink *this* many people?" She gestured at the tens of thousands of words cut into his skin.

"I'm good at persuading lines from lone sailors who're too frightened or confused to tell anyone afterwards. Even though their rhymes don't usually make much sense."

"Maybe they don't make sense because they're frightened!"

He shrugged. "I'm also good at listening to people who don't know I'm there, listening to their conversation and their music, gathering anything which sounds convincing."

"But why do you *need* rhymes?"

Tangaroa frowned. "Our elders believe these rhymes will help us find our way home, to the island where our ancestors were born. Our ancestors navigated using rhyming word trails, and our tribe hope that if we listen hard enough, we will find the true words to lead us home."

"How can words be used for navigation? Don't you need compasses and maps?"

"No. Long before the electronic instruments your sailors use, before even instruments for north-seeking and star-reading, sea people used descriptions of shorelines, currents and swells to remember and pass on journeys.

"Words can be easier to pass on than maps. If I wanted to guide you to that smaller cave, I'd say: stand up, walk ten paces to your right, follow the cave wall to your left until you come to an arch, then walk down the tunnel. That would get you there much faster than a map, because with a map you have to work out where you are, how to orientate it and what the scale is."

Helen nodded. "But why in rhyme?"

"Because directions from one side of the world to the other are long, and rhymes are easier to remember."

"Surely maps are more accurate for long distances?"

"Not if we don't know the modern map name of our island. We come from the largest ocean in the world, with many thousands of islands."

"Why don't you just reverse the instructions which got you here?"

He looked embarrassed himself now, pink tingeing the edges of the blue patterns on his cheeks. "We got here by accident. Our ancestors were blown far off course, and found themselves in the wrong ocean, with no verses to help them find their way home. We can't reverse the direction, because we don't know how we got here. That's why we gather verses, hoping to find the ones which will get us home."

Helen glanced over at the pool, which was filling up with rising seawater. The tethered rowing boat was higher, and the mermaids' table was floating closer. She looked back at Tangaroa. This was the daftest belief she'd heard since she'd met her fabled friends. How could she be polite about it?

"But, Tangaroa," she said gently, "why do you believe that random rhymes from scared sailors will get you home? How could they possibly know which Pacific island you're from?"

Tangaroa laughed. "Well done, land girl! You've taken five minutes to work out what took me years, and what my tribe still hasn't recognised. I agree. Why should people who've never sailed our home waters have tribal memories of our way home? These rhymes," he slapped his blue arm, "are a distraction. I'm looking for another way home. The deep sea powers must know where we come from. If I win the contest, then serve them well as herald, perhaps they will tell me."

"So you collected all those rhymes to become the blue men's contestant, even though you don't believe in them?"

He nodded. "That's why I'm determined to win. I'm not going to let a seal girl or a fishtail stop me getting home!"

Helen frowned at him. "You're from an island. You have legs not fins. And your elders think human memories can tell you the way home. Are the blue men of the Minch human?"

"Of course. We're as human as you."

"But you live in the sea!"

"We live *by* the sea, not *in* the sea. There are lots of caves on the Scottish coast. Our elders believe we won't find the true way if we move too far from currents and tides. We don't sleep at sea, or tattoo there. We spend less time in the water than the selkies, and much less than the mermaids, but we do consider ourselves a sea people."

"Why don't you freeze in this water, and why doesn't your skin wrinkle and peel?"

Tangaroa lowered his voice. "Seal oil! It makes us waterproof. But don't tell your friend Rona!"

He'd been so open with his answers that Helen asked the question which everyone else had avoided. "Tangaroa, what's the second task?"

He didn't look shifty or change the subject. He just grinned his big fierce grin. "You don't want to know, or you won't think your selkie friend is so cuddly and cute!" He laughed. "But don't worry, you'll find out soon enough."

Chapter 12

Helen still didn't have an answer about the second task, but as the selkies served dessert, she noticed the water had risen even further. Now that the mermaids' table could float closer, she might get answers about her almost fatal hairstyle.

Anyway, she didn't like selkie puddings. They were too salty. She got up from the bench and sat right at the edge of the water. Yann stood behind her. Helen was glad he was there. It was daft to be more nervous about speaking to mermaids than about sitting beside blue loons. There was no real evidence the mermaids meant her any harm, whereas the blue loons had definitely tried to tip her out of a boat.

Maybe that's why she was nervous. The blue loons were dangerous, but they were completely open about sinking boats. Whereas if the mermaids *had* tried to drown her, they were now simpering like it had never happened.

Rona sat beside Helen. "I've spent all three fish courses listening to everyone's top tips for winning the Sea Herald contest, so I asked them all if they saw the mermaids leave during the speeches. No one saw any guest leave the feast."

"But if no one left this cave," Helen said, "how could someone have attacked me? Is that tunnel the only way into the small cave?"

"Seawater gets in and out of the side cave through a wide crack in the rock. So any sea being who could squeeze through a hole *this* size ..." Rona's hands drew a circle a little wider than her shoulders, "... could get in from the open sea."

Helen looked at the mermaids. "When the water was lower, their table was further from the crowd, nearer the sea arch. So perhaps a few mermaids could have gone out to sea and into the other cave without anyone noticing."

Helen raised her voice. "Serena? Can we chat?"

The mermaids swished their tails, and the table floated over. When it settled against the floor of the cave, Serena was nearest to the fabled beasts, her delicate chin resting in her hands.

"What a SHAME! What HAPPENED to you, my dear human girl?"

Helen asked cautiously, "What do you think happened?"

"Your hair is so UNTIDY again! Did you take it out yourself? Did you not LIKE what we did?"

"I was happy with the plaits," said Helen, "but I didn't like the hair accessory."

"What accessory? We used twisted kelp fibre to tie the plaits. Quite unobtrusive in your EARTHY brown hair."

"I mean the heavy chain which I was tied to and left to drown ..."

"Oh my GOODNESS! How AWFUL! What a SHOCK for you. Who would DO that to your LOVELY hair? And to you of course ..."

Helen stared straight into Serena's sea-blue eyes, and kept staring, without answering, until the mermaid glanced away.

Then Helen said, "I have no idea who did it, Serena. Do you?"

"No! No idea AT ALL!"

"Was anyone in the cave when you left?" asked Yann in a friendlier voice.

"GOODNESS no," answered Serena with a huge smile. "We left your sleeping beauty QUITE safe on her own when Strathy summoned us."

She turned to the other mermaids. "Orla, Inigo, Zenna, does ANYone remember ANYthing? A LOOMING presence perhaps, a MURDEROUS shadow, a MYSTERIOUS line of bubbles under the water, a GLOWING trail of slime on the wall?"

Yann snapped, "Please take this seriously. Helen nearly died!"

"My DEAR, we ARE being serious. If we think of ANY clues, we will OF COURSE let you know."

Yann muttered something about pretty faces being no substitute for useful answers, while Catesby chattered a question.

"A motive? Surely that's OBVIOUS, dear bird." Serena glanced at Helen, and said, in a voice that was suddenly hard and gravelly, "Someone resents your dryshod friend's polluting human influence on the selkie contestant and is trying to remove her." She shook out her hair and smiled a shiny smile. "After all, not EVERYONE loves humans as much as WE do."

The mermaids drifted away, navigating their floating feast past young selkies playing in the water.

Helen wrapped her arms round her knees. "Rona, does someone resent you having a human friend? Does someone think you're more likely to win without me here? Or is someone trying to stop you winning?"

"That makes no sense," said Lavender, whirring beside their ears. "Someone tried to stop Roxburgh winning earlier. Surely someone isn't trying to stop Rona as well?"

Helen rubbed her eyes, her salty fingers making them sting. "I'm too tired to think. If we don't go home soon, I'll be too tired to row."

The mermaids giggled at Yann's wobbling attempts to board the boat, until it was steadied from the water by four selkie children. Then Helen rowed out of the cave, with Yann crouched even lower because the high tide made the archway smaller, and Rona guiding her friends back to the mainland.

"So Rona," Helen panted, "tell us about the race. How far do you have to swim?"

"Whatever distance it is," Yann interrupted, "you have to choose one of two strategies, Rona. Either get in the lead immediately and stay there, or hang back, let the others do the work at the front, and save your energy for a sharp sprint at the end. You have to choose. Don't fudge it. Don't start at the front then slip back, because whoever overtakes you already feels like the victor and you already feel defeated."

Rona sighed. "It's a race, not a battle, Yann."

"Where do you start?" Helen asked. "Will we be able to watch?"

"If you stand on the ridge of the island an hour after dawn, you'll get a good view of the start. You won't see much else until we get back, and I've no idea how long that will take, because the race isn't just about speed, it's about dealing with hazards. We have to swim through a wreck, cross a rock run, then reach the furthest point of the course, and cross the tidal race on the way back."

"What's the furthest point?"

"The closest fishing boat. We have to swim right along its length, on the surface, close enough to touch the hull."

"That's really stupid!" Lavender said. "What if you're seen? Well, not you, you look like a seal. But what if the mermaid or blue loon are seen?"

Helen frowned. "Even being seen as a seal is dangerous, because fishermen don't like seals near their nets. Rona! What if you're seen and *shot?*"

"I know." Rona's voice was unsteady. "It is risky, but that's the point. Sea Heralds have to be able to cope with all the hazards of the sea when they're delivering their message, which includes boats and humans, so the race tests that. I've been brought up to avoid fishing boats; now I'm being told to swim right up to one."

"How will they know if you do it or not?"

"There are judges at each of the obstacles."

"So if you get into trouble, will they help you?"

"You can request rescue, but if you do, you're disqualified."

"If the judges are there, Rona, you don't have to worry about being injured or trapped. So what are you worried about?" Yann asked briskly.

"I'm worried about panicking. About being scared and refusing to start, or seeing the fishing boat and bolting for home. That's not something you can help me with, Yann, because you're never scared of anything."

Helen was about to reassure Rona, when she heard the centaur's low voice. "I do get scared, Rona. Sometimes. But I don't let it stop me. I know that once I've beaten the fear, I've almost beaten the thing I'm afraid of."

Catesby asked a question in an amazed tone.

"What am I scared of? I'm not keen on small boats sitting on top of large amounts of water. Flying on a dragon's back isn't easy for a centaur either. Standing on the doorstep of a human house was terrifying too. In fact, most of the things I do with our human friend scare me, but I do them anyway. So Rona," his voice was gentle, "focus on us cheering as you finish first, and the fear will melt away. You'll be great."

Rona said shakily, "Will you all be there tomorrow? To see me come home?"

"I'll be there," said Helen, "but what if Lavender and Catesby blow away?"

"No storms will be sung tomorrow morning, so if you stay in the shelter of the old farmhouses, and if Lavender doesn't fly too high, you'll be fine."

Catesby added a couple of proud squawks, and Rona laughed. "Two new adult feathers? One on each wing?

So if Lavender does get blown away, you can fly after her and catch her! That's the jetty, Helen. Can you see it?"

Helen twisted round and saw a camping lantern in the distance. "We're fine from here. You go and get a good night's sleep."

Rona gave each of them a tight hug, then undid her sealskin, flicked it into the air, and dived, wrapping the cloak around her. By the time she hit the black water, she was a seal.

Helen waited until Rona was out of earshot, then said to Yann, "That was nice of you to admit being scared sometimes."

"It wasn't true, obviously. I just said it to make her feel better. I'm never actually scared."

Helen smiled, and rowed the last hundred metres to the shore.

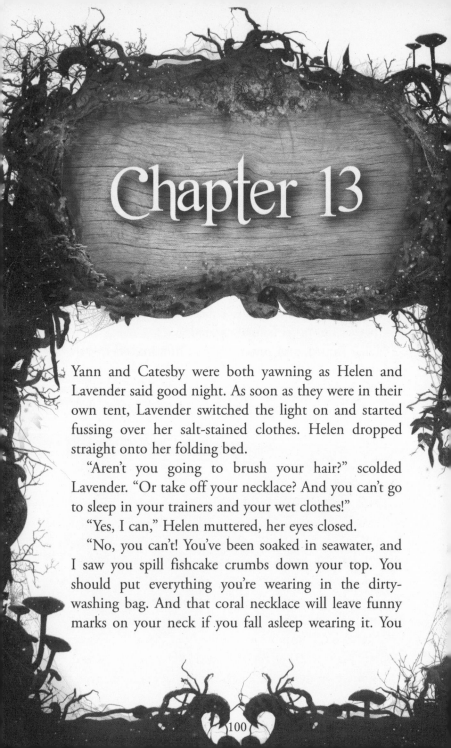

Chapter 13

Yann and Catesby were both yawning as Helen and Lavender said good night. As soon as they were in their own tent, Lavender switched the light on and started fussing over her salt-stained clothes. Helen dropped straight onto her folding bed.

"Aren't you going to brush your hair?" scolded Lavender. "Or take off your necklace? And you can't go to sleep in your trainers and your wet clothes!"

"Yes, I can," Helen muttered, her eyes closed.

"No, you can't! You've been soaked in seawater, and I saw you spill fishcake crumbs down your top. You should put everything you're wearing in the dirty-washing bag. And that coral necklace will leave funny marks on your neck if you fall asleep wearing it. You don't care enough about your clothes, or what you look like. It's like sharing a tent with a *boy*!"

Helen laughed, and sat up. She'd never get to sleep with Lavender nagging her. She pulled off her shoes and kicked them under her bed, then peeled off her soggy socks and chucked them towards the dirty-clothes bag.

She reached her hands behind her neck, and swivelled the necklace round to bring the clasp to the front. She stood cross-eyed with her chin tipped down to see the stiff catch, as her short fiddler's nails struggled to open the necklace.

Then Helen stopped.

She could see a strand of pink gooey jelly trapped in the silver catch.

Helen jerked at the necklace with both hands.

The cord snapped and coral beads flew all over the tent.

Lavender squealed. "Careful! You nearly knocked me out of the air!"

Helen didn't answer. She just held the broken cord, and the clasp with its lump of goo, out at arm's length.

"Look," Helen said, very quietly. "Look at the clasp."

Lavender swooped over. "Pale pink? That's not really your colour."

"No, it's the colour of the sea-through."

Lavender gasped. "The pouch Rona found was filled with things the sea-through was claiming back for the sea. Coral comes from the sea."

Helen nodded.

Lavender whispered, "Did the sea-through try to reclaim this necklace too? Did the sea-through try to drown you?"

"I think so. It must have squeezed through the sea hole, tied my plaits to the chain, and tried to steal my necklace."

"Then why didn't the sea-through get the necklace?"

101

"It has a really stiff clasp. I only got it off by breaking it. The sea-through must have ripped a bit of skin trying to open it." She shuddered and dropped the clasp on the floor.

"Why didn't it break the necklace if it wanted the coral that much?"

"The sea-through couldn't have broken it without waking me up. Perhaps it thought if I drowned and was underwater, the coral would be back in the sea."

Lavender hovered above the clasp looking at the goo clue. "So this is suddenly more complicated, but also a lot simpler. Simpler because there's only one attacker. You and Roxburgh were both attacked by the sea-through. It's nice to know the mermaids aren't murderers. But more complicated because it makes no sense at all. What motive does the sea-through have for attacking a selkie at the Storm Singer competition, then attacking a human at the Storm Singer feast?"

Helen was scratching her scalp and rubbing at her neck. Knowing she'd been attacked by a sea-through was making her feel much yuckier than thinking she'd been attacked by mermaids. "Maybe it likes ruining selkie events? Maybe it came to disrupt the feast, saw me alone and took the opportunity to drown me and take the necklace?"

Before Lavender could answer, Helen heard a noise outside. Not the rustle of tent fabric, nor the murmur of the sea. A sudden splash and a faint whisper.

"What was that?" Helen bent nearer to the tent wall.

She heard a voice hissing, "Where is she?"

"Did you hear that?" Helen breathed.

Lavender nodded.

"Where is she and that stolen coral?"

"It's the sea-through!" Helen sat very still, Lavender hovered beside her, and they listened.

"Where is that nasty girl who ripped my bag? I'll drown her with her pillow this time. I'll get that coral back before my midnight meeting, even if I have to cut it off ..."

The voice was right outside the tent.

"Who's it talking to?" Helen whispered. "Are there two of them? Two of them wanting to drown me again!" She was shaking. She couldn't decide what to do.

"HIDE!" Lavender said, urgently, right in her ear. "HIDE!"

Helen looked around the tent. She couldn't see anywhere to hide. She was too big to fit behind the rucksacks or the bag of clothes or Lavender's shoebox bed.

So she slid to the floor and crawled under her own bed, catching her hair on the springs under the thin mattress, and squishing herself into the low space, curled up round her wet trainers.

She heard the faint voice whisper outside, "She's not in this big tent. I just see that heavy-hooved horse boy and some sky bird. What about the small tent?" The soft hissing moved nearer.

Helen held her breath.

She heard the tent entrance unzip.

Then Lavender called out in a high voice, "Isn't it nice to have this huge tent all to ourselves, Pansy Petal?" Helen heard her whizzing round the tent, humming to herself.

"I said, Pansy Petal, isn't it nice to have this tent all to ourselves?"

Helen wondered who Lavender thought she was talking to.

Then Lavender said, even louder and more sharply, "And you're very lucky to have that huge bed to yourself, even if it is a bit ridiculous for such a small fairy, aren't you, Pansy Petal?"

Helen suddenly realised who Lavender was talking to. "Oh!" she squeaked, from under the bed, in a tiny fairy voice, "Yes, Lavender. I'm very lucky to have such a big bed!"

She heard the zip creak back up and a soft hiss outside. "Nothing but fabled beasts and fairies in these two tents. The coral thief must be with the other human children. I'll search their tents before my meeting with the selkie."

As the hissing whisper faded, Helen crawled out. Lavender was fluttering, very pale, above her bed. "I saw its eye. Its eye was bigger than me!"

"We have to follow it," Helen said.

"No! It's out there hunting for you! You can't follow it! It might see you, with those big gooey eyes!"

"It might hurt the Scouts if it doesn't find me. And we need to follow it to that meeting, to find out what it's up to."

Lavender shook her head.

"Fine, I'll go myself," said Helen.

"You could take Yann?" Lavender suggested. "He's always up for something daft and dangerous."

"No, getting his attention would make too much noise. Anyway, he's not built for sneaking about. I'll go myself."

"Helen! I can't let you go on your own. I'll have to come too!"

Helen grinned, and unzipped the tent.

She was worried it would be difficult to find a transparent creature in the dark, but as soon as they were outside, they could hear the gentle hiss of its constant commentary, "She's not here ... not there ..."

Once they were round the first row of Scouts' tents, they saw a greeny glow.

Helen took a quick step back, and then peered round the tent again.

The glow was coming from a globe-shaped lantern hanging from the sea-through's fist. When it moved and the light swung round, Helen realised the splashing noise was coming from the globe. It must be filled with water.

The sea-through whispered to the glowing globe. "Driftwood! The sea's beautiful floating wood. Carved and cleaned by the sea, and these savages are going to burn it! We'll rescue it. Take it back to the sea."

The light from the lantern wavered, and Helen saw a fish floating in the water. The glow was coming from a tiny light dangling from its head.

"The sea-through's brought its own torch," she murmured to Lavender.

She watched as the sea-through put the driftwood piled by the Scouts' campfire stones in a huge woven kelp sack. Then it crept up to a tent, held the globe high, and pushed its head slowly through the opening.

Helen gasped.

Lavender chuckled on her shoulder. "It's ok. It's not going to find you! You're not in there."

"I'm not in there, but other people are."

The sea-through's head appeared again. "Boys. Not girls."

It went to the next tent, and peered in. "Yes!" It was whispering very quietly, and Helen had to strain to catch each word, but it didn't seem to have the sense to keep completely quiet. "Yes! Girls! But which one has the necklace? Maybe I should just drown them *all*?"

"It's going to attack them! We have to stop it!" Helen took a step forward.

"No!" Lavender hovered in front of her. "We can't let it know we're here, or we won't be able to follow it to its meeting."

"But we can't let it attack the scouts."

"I know. Let me think."

Helen watched as the sea-through laid the sack and globe down by the tent, and reached inside, its tentacles unwinding.

"Lavender!"

"I'm thinking ..."

"Stop *thinking*, and *do* something, or I'm going to whack it on the head with that driftwood."

So Lavender muttered some soft words and flicked her wand towards the tent. Suddenly there was a giggle from the tent. Then another. Two different high-pitched giggles. And someone said sleepily, "OI! Who's doing that!?"

The sea-through jerked back out of the tent. The giggling got louder, and so did the questions. "Who's ... ha-ha ... who's doing that?" "It's not me ... hee hee ... please stop!"

The sea-through lurched away from the tent, dragging its sack and lantern behind it.

"What did you do?" asked Helen.

Lavender whispered, "Tickling spell. One of my cousins is an expert at them. I'd been saving it to use on Yann. Come on. Let's follow it to that meeting."

So Helen and Lavender followed the glow of the sea-through's lantern, out of the dark campsite, into the night.

Chapter 14

"Ouch!" Helen tried to keep her voice down, but Lavender, floating a few metres ahead, snapped, "Shhh!"

"It's your fault my feet hurt," Helen muttered. "You made me take my shoes off."

They were following the sea-through's sickly green light along the grass above the shore. Then the light changed direction. "It's going down to the sea," Lavender whispered. "We won't be able to follow if the meeting is underwater."

The light wavered and stopped halfway down the beach. Helen could feel round pebbles under her feet as she and Lavender hid behind a rusty boat trailer, watching as the sea-through placed the lantern on the stones. The light glowed through its purple toes and the wriggling tentacles round its ankles. It dropped its big sack, and pulled out the driftwood.

"Back to the wet arms of the sea." The sea-through looked huge in the low-down light, whirling a lump of driftwood round its head and throwing it out to sea. With splash after splash, it threw branches, planks and roots out into the deep darkness.

A voice growled out of the night, "Collecting toys for the sea again, cnidaree?"

"Selkie. You're late."

"Better late than obvious, like you sneaking about at our feast. What a ridiculous idea, trying to speak to me there. At least this is private. Though if you make too much noise playing with your toys, we might gather an audience even here."

"I'm not playing. I am performing my sacred duty. Just as I am part of the bloom, so this wood is part of the sea. I don't ask a reward for doing my duty. Unlike greedy seals, who take from the sea, then demand rewards for giving something back."

"You are just throwing litter into the sea. You do not even know if the sea appreciates it."

"Don't question my sacred duty! You selkies, half-land beings that you are, can never understand."

The selkie chuckled under his breath. "You have a landform too, cnidaree, or how else could you be here, breathing air, talking to me?"

"We're granted this disgusting half-human shape so we can leave the sea to retrieve what belongs to the sea. We don't enjoy it. We don't sing and dance about it like selkies do. But if our equinox plan succeeds, the sea will be able to seize back so much more than we can ever carry."

As the sea-through chucked one last piece of driftwood at the waves, Lavender murmured to Helen, "Which selkie is that?"

"I don't know. We can't see properly unless the sea-through lifts that light up, and I don't recognise the voice. I've mostly met selkies at feasts, speaking loud and clear, not whispering like this. It could be any of the big male selkies ..."

Helen moved round the trailer for a better view, but she couldn't see their faces, just their bare feet and the pebbles.

The low selkie voice said, "Now you have played your games, what do we do next?"

"We? There is no 'we' any more. You and your family failed us."

"We failed *you*? That fiasco today was *your* plan. We did all you asked of us, but it was not enough."

"We have another plan now, and we don't need you."

"But ... but ..." the selkie spluttered, and Helen almost recognised the voice. Desperate to see who it was, she went further behind the metal trailer and clambered onto the tyre, to see if she could get a better view from higher up.

"But ..."

"All we ask of you now is your silence."

"For my silence, will I still get my crown?"

The sea-through laughed. Helen, teetering barefoot on the wheel, grabbed at the edge of the trailer to hold herself up.

"No, you greedy seal. For your silence, you get to keep your life! Not be stung and swallowed! For a crown, you'd need to give us ..." The sea-through's voice dropped so low Helen couldn't hear the next few words.

The selkie answered in a despairing whisper, "I can still help. I still have influence. You could let me ..."

Then Helen's bare foot slipped again on the worn rubber of the old tyre. She jerked forward so she didn't fall off the wheel, and thumped her knee against the side of the trailer. The thud was as loud as a drumbeat.

She heard gasps, then a flurry of splashes.

She scrambled round the side of the trailer, but the lantern had flickered out, and the beach was too dark to see anything. "Light!" she whispered to Lavender. "Light! We need to see who that was."

Lavender lifted her wand. A circle of bright clean lightballs rose up and floated to the edge of the sea.

Helen saw a shiny head disappear under the water. She sighed. That dark fur could be any seal.

Then she looked nearer to the shore. The sea-through had stopped to pick up its globe and empty sack, so it was still in the shallow water. And it was changing.

Under the bright light, Helen and Lavender saw the sea-through's skull and skeleton dissolve into its gooey flesh, as its landform twisted into a circle round its own innards, and then spread out into a bell-shaped lump of transparent jelly round the pale pink belly. The sea-through pulsed off into deeper water, its lacy stings stretching and growing into dozens of thick ropy tentacles, which towed the globe and the sack behind it.

"Yuck!" Helen grimaced. "I thought it was horrible when it was on land!"

"It took much longer to transform than the selkie, which changed so fast we've still no idea who it was," said Lavender.

"But we did hear a lot about their plans." Helen began to limp back towards the campsite.

Lavender snorted. "I'm not sure I know much more than I did. Whatever they were planning today failed, and whatever the sea-through is planning next the selkie can't help with. What else do we know?"

"We know that whatever it's doing, it hasn't given up."

"And we know it doesn't like you, Helen, and it still wants your coral necklace."

"It's not a necklace any more."

"The sea-through doesn't know that. You're still in danger, so I think we should sleep in the boys' tent tonight. Anyway, we need to tell them what we've heard."

Helen muttered, "If we can wake them up."

Lavender laughed. "If prodding them doesn't work, you could fall off something. That makes enough noise."

Helen rubbed her bruised knee. "Or you could tickle them!"

The boys had been too sleepy to understand much the night before apart from the need to stop the sea-through attacking Helen. So in the morning, with cold rain outside the tent and a hot breakfast from Sheila's kitchen inside them, Helen and Lavender showed them the broken necklace and the goo in the clasp, and repeated everything they'd heard.

Even wide awake, no one could make any sense of it.

"What I can't work out," said Lavender in frustration, "is

whether the sea-through's other plan is to do with today's race. If the failed plan was the foiled attack on Roxburgh, is the new plan to attack the Sea Herald contest?"

Helen shrugged. "It didn't talk about the race or the contest. Just about getting stuff back for the sea. But the selkie mentioned a crown. Is there a crown in the Sea Herald contest?"

Yann and Catesby shrugged too.

"The race starts in less than an hour," said Helen. "We have to decide if we're telling Rona what we heard before the race or after."

Yann sighed. "I don't think we should tell her yet. She's nervous enough already. A conversation about sea-through attacks and selkie traitors would not be the best pre-race preparation. She might refuse to compete at all. We should let her race, then talk to her afterwards."

"Shouldn't we *warn* her that the sea-through might be out there?" Helen objected.

"But we have no evidence that it is," Lavender pointed out. "It didn't mention the Sea Herald contest or the race at all."

"She won't be in any danger," said Yann. "There are judges all over the course. They can't help her with the obstacles, but they'd intervene if she was attacked by a huge jellyfish."

Helen shook her head. "I think she has a right to know."

But the others all agreed with Yann, so Helen put the broken necklace in her pocket, and jogged through the drizzle to Sheila's house with their breakfast dishes. The campsite was already empty: the tents and bikes were still there, but the minibuses had gone.

As she stacked the plates in the dishwasher, she asked Sheila, who was making their packed lunches, "Where did the Scouts go so early?"

Sheila didn't turn round, just kept putting sandwiches in bags. "They're climbing Ben Loyal most of the day, taking their canoes out for a quick test run in the afternoon, then having a barbecue tea on the Scout leaders' favourite beach. They won't be anywhere near the race. Rona will be quite safe."

"Thanks, Sheila. And thanks for breakfast." Helen grabbed the packed lunches, and ran out to join her friends.

It was nearly eight o'clock when Helen beached the boat on the gentle eastern end of the island. Yann cantered up the hillside, Catesby flapping by his shoulder. Helen snatched Lavender out of the rainy air and sat the fairy on her shoulder. "Shelter in my hair if you feel the slightest breeze," she ordered as she followed the others.

When she reached the ridge, where the grassy island fell sharply away into cliffs and rocky shore, Yann was already sheltering behind a roofless stone house, so he couldn't be seen from the mainland.

Helen joined him, and stared at the never-ending, ever-moving landscape of the Atlantic stretching to the north. Then she looked at the rocks below, where a crowd of selkies, blue loons and mermaids surrounded the three contestants.

Tangaroa was limbering up on the huge starting rock with extravagant stretches, and whenever he took a break, two of his friends were covering him in protective oil, which Helen hoped wasn't made of seal fat. Serena was perched on the edge of the rock, her tail draped elegantly into the small waves below, while two of her friends were winding her hair round her head. Rona was standing on her own, doing breathing exercises which Helen had taught her.

Yann called down, "Good morning, Storm Singer! Are you singing this rain down on us?"

Rona waved. "No, this is just Scotland in September! The rain makes no difference to us, we'll be underwater most of the race anyway."

Yann turned to his friends. "On three. One, two, three ..." The friends yelled, chirped and squawked, "*Good luck, Rona!*"

Rona waved again, then flapped out her sealskin and became a seal.

"What did she mean, she'll be underwater *most* of the race?" Helen asked. "Won't she be underwater the whole time?"

Lavender perched on her hand and gave her a puzzled look. "She has to come up and breathe. So does Tangaroa."

Helen stood in sudden embarrassed silence, then gabbled, "Of course she does. She's a mammal, isn't she? She's a mammal just like us – not you, Catesby, obviously – but the rest of us. Of course she has lungs, and has to fill them."

Helen shook her head. She was shocked at herself. She'd assumed selkies could breathe underwater. Why didn't she know more about her best friend's seal life? Why hadn't she asked?

"So," asked Helen slowly, "how often will she need to come up?"

"It depends how deep she dives," replied Lavender, "and how long she can spend on the surface recovering, but probably about once every twenty minutes or half an hour."

"What about Tangaroa?"

This time Yann answered. "He'll need to come up for air more often, every ten or fifteen minutes."

"He's human! How can he stay underwater for fifteen minutes?"

"Human free divers can stay under that long without air," said Yann in his lecturer voice.

"How do you know all this?"

Yann grinned and lifted a hoof. "One step ahead of you, as always, human girl."

She punched his shoulder.

"All right! I didn't know until yesterday. I asked the blue loons at my end of the table while you were admiring Tangaroa's tattoos."

"So, Mr Underwater Expert, how often do mermaids come up for air?"

"Never."

"Never? But they definitely breathe in air, or how else do they breathe out to SPEAK like THIS all the TIME ..."

"They have lungs in their chests," said Yann, "but gills in their necks."

"That's why they wear their hair long, even the boys," added Lavender, "because the gills spoil the smooth line of their necks."

Helen felt totally out of her depth. "I thought it was a mermaid's bottom half that was fish, not the top half."

"They're far more than half fish," said Yann. "They're cold-blooded as well."

Helen laughed. "That doesn't surprise me."

As the sun finally broke through the clouds, and the drizzle stopped, Helen looked at Yann, at the huge bulk of his chestnut horse's body and the slim boy's body on top. She wondered if he thought of himself as more than half horse and less than half human.

Catesby squawked, and Lavender said, "They're about to start."

Helen, Yann, Lavender and Catesby watched as a tall mermaid lifted a curved shell and blew a booming note.

Tangaroa dived, Rona and Serena slid, all in one moment, into the cold grey water.

Helen saw three long shapes under the surface speed off to the open sea. Soon they were out of sight, swimming too deep for the friends on the cliff to see them.

"We can't do anything for her now except wait," said Yann.

"And hope," added Lavender. "Wait and hope she comes back safe."

Chapter 15

She watched silver bubbles of air flick off her whiskers as she accelerated through the water. It was always a joy to be back in the sea.

Rona looked to her left, and saw Tangaroa's dark shape, with knives flashing bright at his ankles and a grin flashing white in his face. He speeded up, so she flicked her back fins and propelled her smooth body well ahead of him.

Serena was swimming deeper, and a few strokes behind. The mermaid was harder to see, because she was further from the sunlit surface waters, and also because it was impossible to see long distances underwater. No matter how bright the sun or clean the water, so many tiny plants and animals lived in Scottish seawater that it was never as clear as air. But visibility this morning was as good as Rona had ever seen it, so she'd certainly notice if either of her rivals tried to get ahead.

She settled into a slight lead over the other two, wondering if they could keep this sprint up for as long as she could. Her whole body was ideally evolved to swim underwater. Serena was half perfect and half awkward in the sea. The mermaid had a stronger tail than Rona, but her heavy human head and poky elbows weren't streamlined. Tangaroa's long limbs were better adapted for running or climbing trees than swimming, but he had strong arms and wide shoulders, and he'd been training for this for years.

Anyway, for Rona, the real challenge wasn't beating the mermaid and the blue loon, it was beating her fear of the hazards.

The first obstacle was a wreck, which all selkie pups were warned to stay away from. The rock run and tidal race were dangerous too, but at least they were natural.

She was most afraid of the fishing boat. She couldn't believe her family were encouraging her to get so close to men with nets, knives and possibly guns. Selkies didn't pay much attention to human politics, but they did know that the people most likely to be given licences to shoot seals were fish farmers and fishermen.

Rona felt her pace slow as soon as she thought about the boat. She forced her fins back to a sprint, and stayed comfortably in the lead.

She remembered Yann advising her to start at the front and stay there, or else stay at the back and make her move at the end. Not let anyone overtake her or she'd feel like a loser. So she'd either made her first winning move, or her first major mistake. She was in the lead. Now, by Yann's rules, she had to stay in the lead. She had to face the hazards first.

She felt water shift behind her, and glanced back. Tangaroa was surfacing quickly to refill his lungs. She grinned. She'd be able to stay under for much longer without breathing. Tangaroa kept swimming as he leapt up into the air, breaking the sea's surface like a dolphin, and gasping a chestful of air. He kept his forward motion going beautifully as he surfaced three or four times. By the time he dived under again, he'd lost only a few body lengths to Serena.

The dive to the wreck was only a few minutes away, so Rona knew she should breathe again now, even though she didn't feel the burning need for air.

She'd been impressed by Tangaroa's leaping breath on the move. Seals couldn't just gulp a chestful of air. They needed to breathe long enough to oxygenate their blood then empty their lungs again, so they weren't buoyant.

If only she'd taken this race seriously, she could have practised breathing at a sprint like the blue loon.

She angled upwards. Her snout and whiskers broke the bright surface, her nostrils sprang open and she breathed deeply. She kept swimming along the surface, and after three deep breaths, she forced the final outbreath from her lungs, snapped her nostrils shut, changed the angle of her fins and swam back down. Towards the wreck.

She wasn't in the lead any more. Now she was shoulder to shoulder with Tangaroa.

Where was the mermaid? Still behind, but lower down, so she wasn't much further from the wreck.

Rona looked at the dark water beneath her, water where almost no sunlight reached.

Then she saw a shadow flick past her, upwards.

She flinched. Shark? Whale? No. It was the blue loon. Having looked at the depth they had to dive, he was going to breathe again.

Rona hesitated. She didn't want to lose the lead, but she didn't want to dive to the wreck first either.

Serena didn't overtake when Rona slowed. Perhaps she was going for the second, sneaky one of Yann's strategies. Stay back, let others set the pace, then sprint at the end.

Rona wished Yann was here. Or Helen. Or Lavender. She wanted to do this in a team. But this wasn't an adventure with friends; this was a race against rivals.

So Rona dived.

Her eyes adjusted to the dimmer water. She could see much better in underwater dark with her seal eyes than in overwater dark with her human eyes.

She saw the long fish-like shape of the wreck, the broken propeller lying like a sharp flower on the seabed, the lazy waving of the green and yellow flag which the mermaid judge was shoving in the silt to mark the way into the ship.

Floating above the wreck were two more judges: a selkie she didn't know and a blue man. All three judges were watching to make sure the contestants swam inside the wreck from stern to bow, rather than using the rusty holes in the deck to escape early; and waiting to rescue the contestants if they got into trouble, then disqualify them immediately.

Rona had never been inside this wreck. Teenage

selkies sometimes sneaked in for a dare, and returned with creepy stories of sailors' bodies floating in the water, white hands reaching out to grab seal fins.

In the bright cave, Rona laughed at these stories. But even if she didn't believe the descriptions of bony hands and empty eye sockets, she knew that real live predators liked the small spaces of human wrecks. A shark or a killer whale wouldn't fit in the wreck she was swimming towards, but an octopus or an eel would be very comfy inside.

It was a big wreck. A long swim with no air. They had to enter by the hole for the propeller shaft at the back of the boat, then find their way through the wreck to emerge at the jagged hole bashed in the front.

She was almost at the flag marking the entrance. Tangaroa and Serena were still behind her.

If she went in first, she'd have to use her eyes, her ears, her whiskers, her sense of direction to find her way through. She'd have to be the trail blazer.

She realised she wanted someone else to go first. She didn't care if they gained a tactical advantage by overtaking her. Rona suddenly slowed. Serena and Tangaroa both slowed too, staying behind her, perhaps wondering if she'd seen something inside the wreck.

Rona knew if she stopped dead to force someone else to go first, she would look and feel like a coward. So Rona twisted in the water, used all four fins for a burst of acceleration and forced herself through the small round hole into the wreck.

It was suddenly darker, and the water felt wrong: oilier, less alive, as if it didn't move about as much.

Rona was squashed by the feeling she sometimes

got sleeping on Helen's bottom bunk: stuck in a small unfamiliar space, with corners to bang your head on if you moved too fast, and the suspicion there were monsters under the bed ...

She had to keep going. She pushed through the narrow entrance and found herself in a larger space, where the water tasted even nastier on her lips. A little light was leaking in where the ceiling had collapsed, so she could see enough anemone-covered machinery to know this was the engine room.

Rona pushed herself forward carefully. She saw a couple of staircases nearby. But she needed to get to the other end of the ship, so she sprinted towards the far end of the room, even though she could barely see it. As she got closer, she could make out the steps of another staircase ahead.

When she glanced back, she could no longer see where she'd come in, because her flicking fins had disturbed rustflakes and silt off the floor. She couldn't see Serena or Tangaroa either. Was she in here alone?

She peered through the gloom. She caught a glimpse of the mermaid's red hair, and a little further back, a blue blur. They were all inside the wreck.

Rona sprinted for the wide staircase. She'd never swum up stairs before, but this was easy. Just a push off the bottom step and she glided up a claw's width above the metal treads.

At the top, she found her way out of the huge engine room, into corridors and smaller rooms.

Rona started to hum inside her head, keeping the beat with her fins as she swam down the middle of a barnacle-encrusted tunnel. The door at the bow end was warped and rusty. She turned round and saw Serena dart in at the stern end of the corridor.

Rona battered her hard swimmer's body against the closed door. It didn't budge. She glanced back again. Serena was floating, serenely, at the other end, waiting for Rona to open the door for her. Rona growled, and looked around. There was a half-open hatch above her head. She checked on Serena. The mermaid was too far away to see the hatch. Rona bit down on a grin, mimed an exaggerated shrug of disappointment, then swam back towards the mermaid. Serena smiled, and turned to go out, to be the first to find another way. As soon as she was out of sight, Rona made a lightning quick turn in the water, and shot up and through the hatch.

Now she was in a long room with a pile of white bones in the corner. The sailors! And their fingers! The pile of bones was at the bow end of the room, so she had to swim towards it. Rona shuddered, her fur twitching all along her spine, and swam very slowly towards the pokey heap.

Was it really a pile of skeletons?

She wanted to close her eyes as she glided over. But she couldn't help looking down.

It was a pile of chairs. A pile of broken legs, arms and backs. Bent metal tubes covered in white plastic, which nothing alive wanted to stick to. She gulped an airless laugh. All those teenage selkies, scared of some furniture!

She pushed through a swinging door into a tiny kitchen, where a sudden movement made her jerk sideways. A large and angry octopus sprang out of a dark corner. Rona swerved up to the ceiling then dived for the door, getting out of its lair.

She had come up enough floors now. She needed to push forward. She found another corridor and sprinted up it, fins lashing from side to side. She pushed open another door, and was hit by two floppy black rubber suits and a metal tube. Divers' gear, she thought, as she let them float out of her way. She tried the next door along.

Then she was aware, as she always had to be, of water movement behind her. Was it the octopus from the kitchen coming after her?

No, it was Tangaroa, swimming out of a doorway, joining the corridor halfway up. As she turned another corner, Rona could see the sharp edges of a jagged hole ahead, ripped in the ship by a human bomb, or a rock, or another boat. She didn't care what had made the hole, she only cared that it was her way out of this nasty rusty box. She glanced round. Serena was behind her too, looking irritated at falling for Rona's trick earlier on. They had all found the way out.

But Rona was in the lead. She accelerated, as if she was about to snap her jaws on a mackerel, and she shot out of the gap.

As soon as her head and shoulders were in the clear sweet water of the open sea, she saw an unmistakable pattern.

Black and white. Clear black background. Sharp white oval. The markings of ...

Rona twisted in the water and dived straight back into the wreck.

Those were the markings of a killer whale. The only thing every selkie feared more than a fisherman with a gun. Because killer whales hunt and catch and *play* with seals before ripping them to bloody shreds and eating them.

"Killer whale!" she warned Tangaroa and Serena.

Could a killer whale get through the hole? No, she decided, not a fully grown one. So she didn't flee far. Just a body length away from the open sea.

Tangaroa pushed gently past her and peered out, then turned back to her. He couldn't speak to her. Human voices don't carry underwater, and anyway he'd lose too much air. He must be almost at the limit of his ability to hold his breath.

Rona was about to ask if that air bottle she'd dodged would be any use to him, but the blue loon grinned, raised his eyebrows in amusement, then swam out of the hole and straight towards the killer whale.

Then Serena pushed past her too.

Were they trusting that their human shapes would keep them safe? Rona hoped not, because she'd heard tales of selkies attacked by killers when they were changing from seal to human.

Rona looked out nervously, and saw Serena's tail flick upwards. Safe. Heading for the next obstacle.

Rona also saw a black and white flag, marking the exit point, waving in the water. Looking nothing like a killer whale, except to very nervous selkies.

She heard mermaid laughter in the clean open sea.

Laughing at her? Because she was scared of a flag? Or because she was now in last place?

Chapter 16

Left alone in the sunken ship, Rona wanted to go straight back home. She couldn't win now. She'd never find the courage to face the other hazards.

She thought about her friends waiting on the ridge, her family waiting on the shore, and realised she was more nervous about going home early, and admitting she'd been frightened of a flag, than she was about the rest of the obstacles. So she swam out of the wreck and followed the mermaid towards the rock run.

She let the rhythm of swimming clear her mind. After a few minutes, she surfaced for another breath. Breathing at a sprint was getting easier with practice.

Rona felt the mood of the sea as she swam. She felt the stillness of the sea, the weight of slack water just hanging there. The tide was about to turn, about to rise.

That was the worst time to cross the next obstacle.

The rock run was an oval shelf of rocks: like a small island, but only above the water at low tide. When the tide turned, the water rushed to cover the rocks, so crossing in the next few minutes meant the fast water could drag her off, or crash her into the rocks. But once the tide was high, the rocks would be completely underwater, and quite safe to swim over.

Rona swam at ferocious hunting speed after Tangaroa and Serena, hoping if she proved herself in open water, her mistake in the wreck might be forgotten.

As she finally caught sight of them ahead of her, she felt the tide turn.

She'd tried to explain the turn of the tide to Yann once, saying it was as if all the blood in her veins shifted like a magnet to point the other way, as if twice a day the north pole moved to the other side of the world. It was hard to explain to a land-bound centaur that she *always* knew, without thinking about it, where the tide was. Now she felt it change.

Suddenly in the space of one heartbeat, the tide was going in. The sea was no longer hanging there, waiting. It was rising. Rushing and racing and chasing inland.

They were nearly at the rock run. Rona had almost caught up. She really was faster than the other two in clear water.

Would she be faster over the rocks? Tangaroa, with feet and hands, could run across, and hold on when the waves hit him. Serena also had hands, and if she wanted to waste time and pain changing to human legs she could walk too.

Rona wondered if she should change. Which would

be more useful, her human hands to hold herself on, or her seal's body to protect herself if she was swept off?

She thought about it. There wouldn't be enough water on the rocks to swim over. As a seal she'd have to haul out and pull herself over sharp stone. Even if she lost a minute at either end changing shape, she'd still be faster on feet than fins.

As she made that decision, all three of them were on the surface, swimming in a tight line towards the rocks.

They could see wild splashes climbing up the rocks, in the sea's desperate urge to get higher and higher. They saw a selkie judge clinging to the green and yellow flag showing the starting point on the western side. Rona caught a glimpse of the black and white finishing flag on the east side of the obstacle, which looked nothing like the markings of a killer whale out in the open air.

They reached the rocks together. Rona dived underwater, dived out of her sealskin, and surfaced again as a girl. She used her strong bendy fingers to pull herself onto the rocks, then spent a minute folding her skin and tying the flippers into straps so she could wear it on her back.

Rona stood up. Tangaroa was well ahead, running steadily, but as she took her first few steps, ankle-deep in surging water, she saw him being knocked off his feet by a strong wave.

Serena was trying to swim over, flopping from one shallow dip to another. Tangaroa was up again, powering his way forward. But Rona didn't think he'd chosen the best way. He'd just charged straight across, taking the shortest route.

Instead Rona ran round the southern edge of the rocks. The water was battering into the northern seaward side, but by the time it reached the landward side, the waves had been slowed by the uneven rocks, and were slightly less violent.

This way was longer, though, and it still wasn't easy. She staggered round the slippery rocks, using her hands to grab the jutting points, gasping as the waves battered into her.

She reached for the next rock, but a wave hit her first. She thrust her hands out and felt the stone graze her thin human skin. She clung on tight, as the water crushed her against the rock. Once the wave had passed, she looked to her left. The mermaid was behind her and the blue loon was ahead, but she didn't really care any more, she just wanted to be a seal, not a girl on this horrible smashing together of land and sea.

She flung herself forward again.

Then she was knocked over by something more solid than a wave. And she was in the water, sinking as she always did when she had legs. She expected her human body to welcome the sea, to roll and float, but it never did.

She grabbed the water with her awkward hands and kicked with her flimsy legs and dragged herself back to those awful rocks.

What or who had knocked her off? As she pulled herself up, long hair in her eyes, her pathetic human lungs coughing, she saw the answer. Tangaroa was pulling himself up beside her.

"Do you need a hand?" he asked as he stood up.

"No, thanks, I've got two of my own at the moment. And legs too." She grinned at him, leapt up into the knee-high water, and began to run. He was behind her now, following her route round the edge.

She had the hang of it at last. Waiting for the gaps in

the surging water. Using the rocks to pull herself along.

She could hear Tangaroa splashing and grunting behind her. Where was the mermaid? Rona glanced back. Serena had changed at last, and was halfway across, long legs shivering in the cold water.

With one last lunge Rona reached the flag, and nodded to the blue man judge, who was indicating the direction of the next obstacle.

Rona could go back in the water now. But not as a girl. She had to waste time changing again. Tangaroa dived in past her, while she stopped to pull the folded skin from her shoulders. She'd tied the knots well. One tug, and the skin opened up. She whirled it round in the spray, and pulled it over her as she dived into the water.

Ah! A seal again.

She always closed her eyes at the moment of change; she didn't want to see her hands turn into fins. Even with her eyes closed, she could feel her legs and arms getting shorter, her fingers and toes linking and lengthening, her back getting more flexible, her awareness of the smell and taste and feel of the water sharpening.

Now she was back in lovely deep water. But not in the lead. Rona wanted to catch up with Tangaroa, get ahead of him, because for the first time, after that exhilarating crossing of the rocks, she actually wanted to win.

So she sprinted, right up to Tangaroa.

As she overtook him, she heard the sounds of the next obstacle. A noise like claws on wet rock, magnified a thousand times. The screechy scratchy metal sounds of engines, winches, radios, sonar. The fishing boat.

Rona was going as fast as she could towards humans who might be legally entitled to shoot her if they saw her.

She wanted to turn back. It would be more sensible, safer, to turn back. But she kept swimming forward until she needed to breathe again. She had breathed a lot as a girl on the rocks, but her human body didn't store oxygen as effectively as her seal body. She should fill up again.

She swam up to the surface. Tangaroa popped up beside her. He didn't do his leaping breath. He stopped. So did she. Two dark heads bobbing in the water, looking at the fishing boat a hundred metres ahead of them, its long red hull pointing straight at them.

"Sorry about knocking you off the rocks," he said. "You might have been in front if I hadn't. So you can swim along the boat first."

"That's very kind of you, to send me in first again!" she snorted. "Are you scared of it too? It's only seals they shoot, not people."

He smiled. "Five miles offshore, they're more likely to think I'm a seal than a boy. It's not safe for me either."

"We could go together," Rona suggested, suddenly feeling the ordeal would be more bearable with a companion.

He looked at her sympathetically. "Scared of doing it on your own?"

She nodded.

He smiled. "I'm not looking forward to it myself." Then he shook his head. "But I think both of us together would be more dangerous. We'd be more likely to be spotted."

"We could do it together, but from different ends," suggested Rona. "One from the bow to the stern, the other from the stern to the bow, then even if they spot us, we might confuse them. Give them two targets instead of one."

He thought for a moment. "Ok. I'll swim underwater to the stern, you head slower to the bow. Once we're both in position, we can swim the length of the hull towards each other."

Rona took a deep breath. "Why are we putting our lives at risk like this?"

"Because the race isn't just to test our speed, it's to test our bravery. The Sea Herald needs to be brave."

Rona muttered, "Then you're welcome to the job," but as Tangaroa was already diving, swimming deep and fast to the other end of the fishing boat, she didn't think he heard her.

As she got closer, Rona could see the scarred and dirty underside of the boat, and, more dimly, its huge nets hanging low in the water behind it, half full of panicking fish. Why wasn't it moving forward, trawling for more fish? Perhaps they were about to pull the nets up.

Rona glimpsed three judges floating in a semicircle on the surface, far enough from the boat to be safely invisible.

She was in place now, and she could see the dark shape of Tangaroa at the stern. She flicked a fin, and he waved back.

They both swam to the grey surface, and with heads just above the water, they swam towards each other.

Rona kept her eyes fixed on the boy, trying to ignore the red painted boat to her left. She was concentrating on swimming. Fast, but not so fast that her head rose up high. And she was listening. Not to the sounds of the boat, but to the sounds of the men.

"Time for a cup of tea?"

"Aye, put the kettle on before we pull that lot up."

It was terrifying to hear the men's voices so close, but

reassuring that they were yelling about cups of tea, not seals and guns.

She was about to reach Tangaroa. He didn't have his usual stupid grin, and the blue of his skin was almost invisible in the grey sea. She hoped her fur, dark with water, was as hard to see. They passed each other in the middle of the boat's length, too nervous to nod, and both swam as fast as possible along the rest of the hull.

The voices were even louder as Rona headed for the stern, where the winding gear was. She wanted to dive, to be safe in the depths of the sea. But the judges were watching her, and Tangaroa was staying on the surface. She had to stay here, in view, in danger.

She was swimming under the ship's name now: "Sea Quine, Peterhead". Then she was past the stern, with open sea either side.

She emptied her lungs to dive, and heard a voice yell, "Did you see that?"

But Rona was already diving deep to get down and round the poisonously bright blue nets.

She was shaking with relief, struggling to swim in a straight line, her front flippers out like wings to keep herself steady. She'd done it. She'd swum right beside a fishing boat. Surely nothing else in the Sea Herald contest could be that scary.

She turned round, to convince herself that she had done it, and glimpsed Serena's silver tail flicking along the surface. The mermaid hadn't stopped for a chat, and she was now only a couple of minutes behind. So Rona swam forward to keep up with Tangaroa, to try to win this race.

Then, over the screeching and creaking of the boat, she heard a scream.

Chapter 17

Rona felt the water swirl as Tangaroa turned to look back too.

But there was no shot reverberating through the water. No one had attacked the mermaid. She simply hadn't dived deep enough after swimming along the ship, and her tail was tangled in the empty upper half of the net.

Serena had only screamed once. She was now struggling to free herself, but those useful human hands weren't strong enough to pull her loose.

Rona glanced over at the mermaid judge. None of the judges could help, not unless Serena asked. And Serena wasn't going to ask. She was thrashing to get free, tangling herself up more.

Rona shook her head. She didn't really need to win

this race. She'd proved she was faster than the blue loon and the mermaid. She'd proved she wasn't a complete coward. She didn't need to prove anything else.

So she flicked over to Tangaroa, and said, in her underwater seal voice, "Lend me a knife, please!"

He frowned at her, then reached down to his left ankle and pulled out a knife. She slid out of her sealskin, rolled it up under her arm, and reached out her human hand for the knife. He gave it to her, shrugged, and swam away. Fine, thought Rona. He could win. He could be Sea Herald. She was a Storm Singer, she didn't need any other titles.

She would need a breath of air in her human lungs soon though, so she'd better cut that mermaid out fast.

Rona swam back to the net, where Serena snapped, "I don't NEED help. They might disqualify me!"

Rona couldn't use her human voice underwater, so she ignored Serena and started hacking through the thick ropes.

"CAREFUL! Don't cut me!" Serena's piercing sea-voice carried through the water perfectly.

Rona just kept sawing at the ropes, one strand at a time.

"Not THAT careful! You're not cutting FAST enough. He's getting away."

There was a sudden rusty whine, the net jerked upwards, and Rona's knife slipped. The blade slid into the mermaid's tail.

"AHHHH! You CUT me! You INJURED me! You're trying to SABOTAGE my race!"

There was another screeching whine and another short jerk.

Rona was sawing as fast as she could, because that

whine meant the winch had started. The net was about to be pulled up into the boat. Soon the mermaid would be hauled out of the water and the fishermen would see her.

Rona couldn't cut the net fast enough. Serena had thrashed about so much, the ropes were tightly knotted round her tail. As Rona looked at the number of strands she still had to cut, the net jerked again and the mermaid rose higher. Rona didn't think she was going to cut her free in time.

Then she felt the water shift to her left and saw the flash of another knife. Now she was cutting the net at one side of the tail, a blue hand was cutting the net at the other side, and the knives were moving towards each other.

There was a louder whine and a jerk which became a gradual upward pull. The net began to rise steadily out of the water. But the blades met in a scrape of silver and the net came apart. The mermaid swam out and all three of them sprinted away.

They surfaced a minute later. Rona took a gulp of air, and handed Tangaroa back his knife. She spun in a circle, looking for the mermaid.

Serena was nowhere to be seen.

"She didn't even come up to say thank you!" Rona spluttered.

"You'll wait a long time for sincere thanks from a mermaid," said Tangaroa. "But I'll thank you, for making this a much more interesting race than I'd expected. Can we catch her up?"

"Oh yes." Rona slipped back into her sealskin and grinned, showing all her sharp teeth. "Your knife slipped when I was cutting round her tail, and she's injured.

She won't be moving as fast as usual. So I'm sure we can catch a fish!"

They both dived, and swam towards the last obstacle. The tidal race.

Rona and Tangaroa caught up with Serena easily. The mermaid was flicking her tail unevenly, a thin line of blood leaking from the scales on her right side. Rona grimaced, and called to Tangaroa, "I didn't do it deliberately!"

The dark pair overtook the pale mermaid, and headed for two islands close together by the shore. In the gap between the islands was a vicious tidal race, where fast-moving water battled to get through the narrow, shallow space.

Rona and Tangaroa were no longer swimming side by side to be companionable, they were sprinting as fast as they could. Whenever Rona accelerated, Tangaroa kept pace with her. He had huge amounts of stamina.

Rona felt the pressure and tension of the water increase as the seabed shelved up towards the shoreline.

As they approached the two rocky islands, Rona could see the bright blonde hair of a mermaid judge, keeping well back from the currents.

Rona and Tangaroa both swam upwards to breathe.

The surface of the sea was calm. An oily shiny calm. Not quite flat, but a field of greasy humps, slipping around each other, like snakes under a silk scarf. The lack of waves and spray made the narrows look gentle, but to experienced coastal swimmers like Rona and Tangaroa, it showed the power and turmoil underneath. It would be like swimming through an underwater storm.

"Have you swum through this before?" gasped Tangaroa.

Rona shook her head. "It's deadly. Take a current wrong and it can knock you unconscious. Lose your bearings and you can swim to the seabed and never come up. But we have to do it."

"I have to do it. Because I want to win. You don't have to. Not if you value your life more than being Sea Herald."

"Don't you?"

"Being Sea Herald *is* my life, Rona, because it's my way home. See you on the other side." He dived down and into the narrows.

Rona knew she had to follow immediately, or he would get too far ahead. She didn't have much courage left. But she had done the fishing boat. Twice. She could do the tidal race. It was only water, after all.

She took a gulp of air, emptied her lungs and dived.

The view under the surface was just as calm. She couldn't see the currents or the riptides, not even with a seal's seagoing eyes. She could feel them though, with her whiskers, her fur, with every part of her sea sense.

The currents were wet ropes of motion, winding round each other, trying to batter each other out of the way, like separate rivers all tied in a knot. Not mixing, not flowing into each other; staying in their own streams. Fighting to get between the islands to the coast first.

Before she'd even flicked her fins to force herself forward, Rona felt a current tug at her back fin.

One stringy little current couldn't stop her, so she darted ahead. Or tried to. But the other fin was caught too. She couldn't move forward.

It couldn't be a current. A current would push or pull you, slip past or batter into you, but it wouldn't cling on to you. Rona somersaulted in the water to see what was winding round her.

She saw a sea-through, in its boneless underwater form. An almost transparent ball in the water, floating close behind her, thick tentacles wrapped round her rear fins. The biggest sea-through she'd ever seen.

She lashed her fins side to side, but the sea-through allowed itself to be wafted through the water. It didn't let go. Its soggy weight held her back, keeping her out of the tidal race.

As she twisted round, she saw Tangaroa, upside down in the whirling currents. He was looking back at her.

She smiled in relief. He'd come and save her, use those knives to threaten the sea-through.

The blue loon looked at her, trapped on the edge of the knot of currents, then shrugged, flipped the right way up, and swam off.

Rona growled furiously. Tangaroa had turned back to help a moaning mermaid, but he wouldn't come back to help her. Winning was too important to him.

Perhaps the blue loon winning was important to this sea-through too. Because if it stopped Rona getting into the narrows, Tangaroa would win the race.

She started to somersault around the sea-through, trying to loosen its stinging grip. It wrapped more tentacles round her back fins, and reached out for her front fins too.

"Let go!" she called through the water. "You have no right to stop me!"

She looked round for the mermaid judge. But she

hadn't swum near enough the tidal race to see Rona on the very edge. If the selkie yelled through the sea for help, she might be disqualified.

So she snarled at the sea-through, "Let go or I'll bite!"

The sea-through's voice rumbled from its guts, "I will not let go."

Despite her threat, she didn't fancy biting this creature. It would taste horrid, it would sting her mouth, and if she bit, it might retaliate rather than just holding her back. How else could she get free?

"Let me into the narrows," she pleaded.

"No. I will keep you here so the sea can get what the sea deserves."

She pulled forward and the sea-through pulled back.

"Then let's go to the judge," Rona said, "and see what she has to say." Rona somersaulted over the sea-through and pulled the other way, towards the out-of-sight judge.

The sea-through started dragging her towards the tidal race, to stop her getting to the judge. As soon as it was pulling Rona where she really wanted to go, she reversed, using her front fins and all her streamlined weight to push backwards, to force the sea-through and herself into the tidal race.

With both their weight pushing the same way, the entangled pair shot straight into the fighting currents.

They were swept into the middle of the tidal race, with no control over their direction or speed. Rona caught a glimpse of Tangaroa ahead, battered by whips of water. She tried to use her free fins to guide herself that way, but the sea-through was holding tight.

Rona sensed a massive twisting chaos of water below

them, so she stopped using her fins to keep her position in the water and dropped like a large blubbery weight, pulling them both into the invisible storm below.

Suddenly it felt like her whiskers were being ripped from her cheeks and her fur from her spine, then the weight of the sea-through really was ripped from her back fins and she was free.

The currents had pulled them apart.

She had lost the sea-through but she had also lost her bearings, and she was being rushed along in a strong wide stream as if she was a lemonade bubble being sucked up a straw.

She struggled to escape, but she was held as tight inside the current as she had been in the sea-through's tentacles. She bunched her muscles, and imagined Yann's legs kicking a door down, Catesby's wings pushing him into the air, Helen's arms rowing the boat, and she used everyone's strength to force herself out of the wide current and into the turmoil around it.

Now her body was being pummelled by lots of smaller currents, which she should be able to force her way through. But she didn't know where to go. With currents to every side confusing her sea sense, it was hard to know up or down, east or west.

Then she saw the blue loon again. Purple-faced, running out of air. Upside down again and windmilling his arms. She swam past him, flicking her fins.

Then she was caught full in the face by another fast current. It slapped her so hard she was flung to the surface of the sea, and swallowed a mouthful of air and water before she could swim again.

But she managed to glimpse the overland shapes of

141

the islands, and get her bearings at last. By the time she had recovered and was swimming in the right direction, the blue loon had surfaced, and swum off too. Then, like a change in the weather, the water was suddenly calmer. Rona was out of the tidal race.

Tangaroa was in the lead. But Rona wasn't going to let him win. Not after he had left her in the tentacles of his nasty pink accomplice. She gathered her last few sparks of energy, and chased the blue loon.

But the tidal race hadn't sapped his ridiculous stamina. He was sprinting for the flags on the shore of Eilan nan MacCodrum, and Rona was exhausted.

She was also furious. She was angry at the sea-through who had tried to stop her, at the mermaid who hadn't even thanked her, at the blue loon who hadn't come back to help her.

This was what her seal body was for. Shooting through the sea, hunting her prey.

She swam faster than she ever had before.

Without fur or whiskers or a seal's underwater senses, the blue loon didn't even know she was catching up. He just kept swimming confidently for the finishing line.

Suddenly, Rona was at his shoulder. She saw the surprise in his eyes. They both found another burst of speed, and raced the waves up the rising seabed to the shore.

Chapter 18

"There they are!" Yann yelled.

Helen shoved the bracelet she'd been threading from the remains of her necklace into her pocket and peered over the edge. "I see two heads!"

"Two *dark* heads," said Lavender. "It must be Rona and Tangaroa! They've left Serena behind."

"It's too close!" shouted Yann. "It's going to be a draw."

Catesby squeaked in excitement.

"One of them is pulling away!" screamed Helen. "But *who is it?*"

A shiny wet body crashed onto dry land just half a second before a blue hand slapped down.

"*She won!*" the four on the ridge all yelled at various pitches. "Rona won!" They leapt around, whacking each others' shoulders and wings. Once they'd calmed down, they looked at the shore again.

Rona was lying in the surf, exhausted. The blue loon had pulled himself further out, and was sitting up, but his head was between his knees, and they could see his tattooed back and ribcage heaving for breath.

"Where's Serena?" asked Helen. "I hope she's alright."

"I hope Rona's alright," said Lavender. "She hasn't moved since she hauled out."

Helen said, "Let's go and see if she needs us."

They slithered down the damp grass to the boat, and Helen found it a little easier to row round the island. Her arms were getting stronger.

As they reached the starting rock, a selkie rose out of the water ahead of them. "Halt your vessel, please. The third contestant is coming in slowly."

They saw Serena's gleaming head and white arms flap through the last six or seven waves and onto the land. She curled up on a rock and sobbed loudly.

"Bad loser," muttered Yann.

"Her tail is injured!" yelled a high voice. "Get the healer!"

Helen jerked her hands to the oars, then realised they didn't mean her. She'd healed her friends' injuries when they were miles from their own families, but she wouldn't be needed here. There were lots of adult mermaids, and anyway, she'd only seen her mum treat a few koi carp, never a fish with a tail as large as Serena's.

The selkie let them pass, so they rowed to the rocks, and jumped out to join Rona. She was now in her girl form, wrapped in a golden sea-velvet blanket, sipping from a green mug.

"Well raced!" called Yann, as he crossed the rocks carefully. "Did you take my advice and leave it right to the end? Let the loon do all the work, then take him by surprise?"

Rona laughed. "Not really. I was in front, then he was in front, then we were neck and neck, then he was in front again, then I got there just in time. Tactically it was bit of a tangle, but it worked in the end."

"Tangaroa swam a good race too," said Yann admiringly, "for someone with no fins or tail."

Rona humphed. "He got a bit of help."

"What?"

She lowered her voice. "I was attacked by the sea-through."

Helen said, "Attacked by the sea-through? Really?"

She glared at Yann, who said guiltily, "Are you alright, Rona?"

"I'm alright now, but it tried to stop me getting into the tidal race. I think it attacked me to help Tangaroa. He saw me struggling and didn't come back and help, even though he helped when Serena was trapped by the fishing net."

Yann muttered, "That's cheating! He should be disqualified for accepting outside help!"

Lavender murmured, "So is the sea-through's plan to help the blue loon?"

Helen said, "Rona, we need to talk to you about ..."

But suddenly a blue hand appeared in their circle and patted Rona on the shoulder. "Congratulations. Well swum, selkie." Tangaroa's voice was a bit croaky, but he sounded sincere.

"No thanks to you, leaving me to be drowned by that

snot monster! You helped a simpering mermaid get free, but abandoned me!"

"What do you mean?"

"You looked back and *saw* me being held on the edge of the tidal race by a sea-through, but you just shrugged and swam away. If winning is more important to you than others' lives, that's your decision. But it does seem unfair that you swam back to save *her* but not me."

Tangaroa looked at the angry faces around Rona. "I'm sorry you think that. I didn't see anything holding you back. I thought you were hesitating, like you did before the wreck, the flag and the fishing boat. I thought your fear gave me a chance to win, so I took it."

"But you looked right at the sea-through, when it had its tentacles round my fins." Rona stretched out her legs to show red weals.

Helen opened her first aid kit.

Tangaroa shook his head. "I'm sorry, Rona, maybe I did look right at it, but sea-throughs are almost transparent. If I looked right at it, I also looked right through it. I didn't know I was leaving you in danger, really I didn't."

Rona frowned. "If you had known, would you have given up the chance to win to help me?"

He bit his blue lip. "I hope so." He turned his back on them and walked off.

As Helen put the last of her cold packs on Rona's legs, Yann said, "Do you believe him? Or do you think he was conspiring with the sea-through?"

"I don't know. He wants to win much more than I do, so perhaps he would ask a sea-through for help." Rona stared after Tangaroa. "I don't want to be beaten by a cheat."

"So are you going to try to win the contest yourself?" asked Yann in excitement.

Rona smiled at him. "I suppose so."

Helen said, "Then we really need to ask you about ..." She was interrupted by a scream.

Rona winced. "That's Serena. I should see how she is, because her injury is sort of my fault." She explained to her friends about the knife cut as they walked towards the group of mermaids.

Serena was lying on the rocks, her head in her arms, wailing at the other mermaids. "But I HAVE to get in the sea! I HAVE to compete!"

The mermaid who'd blown the shell to start the race was dabbing bright green liquid on a long wound in Serena's tail. She said soothingly, "You know you can't take a scale-wound into the sea, Serena, in case infection gets in and gives you tail-rot. You'll have to stay onshore for a week, keep your tail damp with boiled water, and wait for the wound to heal before you swim again. You'll have to resign from the contest."

"No!" howled Serena. "NO! I have to swim. I have to WIN!"

Helen sighed. She looked at Rona, pale and tired after her race, but now determined to win the contest.

"Rona," Helen whispered, "do you mind if I help Serena?"

"Of course not."

Helen stepped forward, considering how to do this without offending the mermaid healer.

"Is that antiseptic?" she asked quietly.

The healer glanced up. "Yes, human child. I'm cleaning the wound. Please step out of my light."

"We clean the scales too," persisted Helen, "before we heal fish."

"We?" the mermaid asked politely.

"I come from a family of healers. My mother sometimes heals fish."

"How interesting that humans treat fish as well as eat them. You are still in my light."

"When she's treated them, my mother lets the fish straight back into the water. They swim again immediately."

Serena looked up at Helen with red swollen eyes.

"How irresponsible," said the healer. "You risk your patients catching water-borne infections."

"Not if you seal the wound," said Helen firmly.

"With what? Cloth bandages? They become waterlogged. Or those sticky pink plasters human swimmers wear? They curl up and fall off."

"We use waterproof sealant to cover the wound, which doesn't need to be replaced for about a week. By then Serena should be growing a white healing skin, shouldn't she?"

The mermaid nodded. "You seem to know about tails and scales."

Helen smiled confidently, though she knew she was acting like Yann, knowing just enough to bluff, pretending more knowledge than she had. She was struggling to remember how her mum had treated a fish hobbyist's favourite carp, but she seemed to be getting away with it so far.

"Do you carry the sealant in your magic bag?" asked the healer.

"DO you? Oh, PLEASE, do you?" pleaded Serena.

"No, but I think I can use something similar. However, Serena, if I find a different sealant, it won't be tested or even completely safe. You have to decide if you want to risk it: it might hurt when I apply it; it might not stay on for very long; it might not protect you as well as staying on land until the white membrane grows. But it will give you a chance to compete. It's up to you."

"PLEASE try. I MUST compete!"

The healer finished applying the green liquid to the silver scales, and looked at Helen. "It is up to her. But I would like to see this sealant."

"I'll have to search for what I need at the campsite," said Helen. "Do you want to come with me on the boat, Serena, or wait for me to row there and back?"

Suddenly they were surrounded by sea folk offering help, announcing that the human healer shouldn't tire herself out rowing, that they would push the boat, and that the mermaid would need cushions to keep her comfy on the way over.

So Helen, the fabled beasts and the pampered mermaid sped across Taltomie Bay, propelled by a ring of chattering blue loons, selkies and mermaids.

Carefully arranged on the bench in the bow, Serena asked Helen in a low voice, "Why are you doing this?"

"Why wouldn't I help?"

"Yesterday you thought I'd DROWNED you."

"Now I know you didn't. Sorry about that."

"TODAY, I'm competing against your friend."

"Why are you all so keen on being Sea Herald?" asked Helen. "It's a dangerous job, and you have to do it for the rest of your life."

"I've ALWAYS wanted to do it."

"Why?"

"Because the deep sea powers have been under the waves longer than anyone else, and if a Sea Herald serves them well, she might be able to find out ..."

"What?"

Serena's tear-stained face twisted angrily. "You didn't see me on the rocks, as your precious selkie and that muscle-bound blue loon ran over them like athletes. I probably lost the race then, because even though I can change my tail to legs, when I walk it feels like I'm treading on hot coals. I can't run, I can only stagger, like a sailor just off a boat. I want legs that WORK. I want to dance, run, climb, and be just as free on land as I am at sea. All mermaids want that."

"Can the sea powers give you that? Do they grant wishes?"

"No. We were cursed to have pain with every step, and only the one who set the curse can lift it. Merras and Thalas must know where that sea witch is now, and how we can persuade her to lift the ancient curse. If I was Sea Herald, I could ask them."

Helen looked at Tangaroa, pushing the boat to shore, who wanted to be Sea Herald to find his way home; at Serena, who wanted to be Sea Herald to lift a curse; and at Rona, swimming by her side, who didn't want to be Sea Herald at all.

As they reached the jetty, Helen leapt out of the boat before it stopped. She asked the willing helpers to carry Serena to the pebble beach, then ran to the racks of bikes between the rows of Scouts' tents.

She searched the saddlebags of three bikes before she found what she was looking for. As she pulled it out, Lavender landed beside her. "What's that?"

"A bicycle repair kit."

"But mermaids aren't bicycles. How will that repair Serena?"

"I can't think of anything else on the campsite which will."

Helen jogged to the gathering on the beach, where she opened the repair kit and her own rucksack, then started laying equipment out.

There was a growing ring of sea people around her, curious about this human child trying to heal a mermaid. Helen had never done first aid with such a big audience before. Lavender noticed her anxious glances, and darted up to Yann, who used his big voice to order, "Give them space!"

The selkies, blue loons and mermaids dived into the bay and swam back to the island, until it was just Serena, the healer mermaid and the group of friends on the beach.

Helen looked at the green fluid. It was darker now, so she touched a fingertip to the tail to check it was dry. "I'm going to try the sealant. Let me know if it hurts. But please stay still. Do you want someone to hold your hand?"

"No, I'm going to be BRAVE. Sea Heralds have to be brave and ruthless, don't they, selkie?"

"Ruthless?" asked Helen vaguely, as she took a tube of tyre glue out of the repair kit.

Lavender shot over. "Glue!" she whispered. "You're going to glue her together?"

"Yes."

"That's ... original. What if the glue's not waterproof?"

"If it's not waterproof it won't be much use for fixing bikes on Scottish roads, will it?"

Helen examined the wound. The cut was deep into the flesh, but not ragged, and only a couple of scales were missing. "I'm going to straighten your tail, protect the wound with the scales, then put the gl— the sealant over the scales. It should keep the water out and be flexible enough for you to flick your tail. Shall I go ahead?"

"Yes PLEASE, human child."

As Helen adjusted the tail and scales, Serena shrieked, "OW! That's sore! You didn't say it would be PAINFUL!"

"Actually she did say it might hurt," pointed out Yann.

"But it's REALLY SORE! You're hurting me deliberately, just like your selkie friend CUT me deliberately."

"I did not!" objected Rona.

"The wound isn't sealed yet," Helen said calmly, "but I'll stop if you want."

"NO! But be more gentle."

Helen squirted glue onto the smooth scales.

"OW! That stings!"

"Just be brave," Yann muttered from behind Helen.

"BRAVE! It's easy for YOU to say brave. She isn't sticking your tail together! OW!"

Serena kept moaning and demanding to know if Helen was finished, as Helen worked her way down the scales.

At last Helen said, "There. I'm finished. Please sit still until it dries. You should be able to swim back to the island in fifteen minutes or so."

"It's still sore, you know. I'm still having to be brave not to cry."

"She's trying so hard, she's forgotten to say thank you," Lavender muttered in Helen's ear.

"So if I can do brave NOW, selkie girl, do you think you can do RUTHLESS after lunch?"

"Now, Serena," whispered the mermaid healer. "Play nicely."

Serena ignored her. "So RONA, have you told your human friend what the second task is yet? Or shall I tell her?"

Helen finished putting everything away. She glanced at the opaque skin on the glue as it dried. Then she looked up. Rona was white. Yann was frowning. Serena was almost purring with glee.

"Alright," said Helen, standing up. "Who's going to tell me?"

Rona opened her mouth, then shut it again.

Serena called out in a cheerful voice, "This afternoon the winner will be the contestant who can SINK the largest number of canoes, and put the highest number of human children in the deep dark northern seas to DROWN. I wonder who will win *THAT* task ...?

Chapter 19

"I can't believe it." Helen stared at the groundsheet, trying not to cry. "That's why your nice friendly Auntie Sheila wanted those Scouts here. That's why no one would tell me about the second task.

"I can't believe you're going to do this, Rona. I can't believe your people do this for every Sea Herald contest. You are going to *drown* children!" Helen looked up. "Rona! That makes you ... a killer!"

Rona spoke softly. "I *am* a killer. I kill fish every day. But this isn't ..."

"You kill fish, but not people. You don't kill people, do you? You're my friend. You're my *best* friend. Have you ever planned to drown me?"

"No, and I'm not ..."

"Stop denying it! Are you doing the task this afternoon?"

"Well ... yes ... but ..."

"Well yes but! That means you're going to try to *kill* those Scouts. I can't *believe* ..."

Helen couldn't say any more. She didn't want to look at Rona, at any of her friends. She had to get out.

"Helen! Please listen ..." Rona's beautiful voice caught in her throat.

Helen stumbled out of the tent, and ran through the deserted campsite.

When she reached the gate, she followed the track inland. She had left the tent without anything. No fiddle, no first aid kit. She was running light, and she sprinted away from the sea, the island, the selkies. She ran until she found a clump of skinny trees bent down behind a low hill. She could still smell the salt and hear the seagulls, but she was out of sight of the sea.

She sat on a twisted tree trunk, and put her head in her hands.

How could Rona do this?

How could Helen have known Rona for so long, and not realise Rona was capable of this?

There was so much she didn't know about her friends. She hadn't even realised Rona didn't breathe underwater until this morning. If she didn't know how selkies' lungs worked, then she couldn't understand how their minds worked.

She didn't know their laws or values either. She didn't know whether they thought killing people was murder or if it was the same as killing herring.

Then Helen wondered about the fishtail she'd healed this afternoon. In a world where people could have fishtails and seals could become people, perhaps the boundaries were blurred.

What was she doing here? Why wasn't she at home, in her village? With humans. Who had rules she knew and understood. Who didn't have strange powers and bizarre competitions with deadly tasks. Who didn't think of a campsite of teenagers as a convenient way to test their ability to sink boats.

Why were Helen's best friends all furred or feathered or four-legged? Why was she here in this odd world rather than texting other eleven-year-olds about film stars and hairstyles?

Why had she just accepted this world? Why hadn't she asked more questions? Though who would have thought to ask: "Do you ever kill people to win contests?"

She should have asked more questions.

But now, she had to save the Scouts.

She tried to remember what Sheila had said. The Scouts were climbing Ben Loyal, then taking a canoe trip before a barbecue tea on a beach. So once they were down the mountain, Helen could intercept them on the road to the campsite, before they took their canoes to the jetty.

"Stop!" she would say. "Don't go out for your afternoon boat trip because a selkie, a mermaid and a boy covered in tattoos are planning to drown you."

That might not work. She'd try to say something they'd believe, something which didn't mention selkies. Because if she betrayed the selkies, the colony would have to leave, and Helen wasn't sure she wanted that. Not if she could get a promise from them never to attack humans again.

She clambered up to the verge and looked along the track. No sign of minibuses with bright canoes on their roofs.

Canoes. On the minibuses.

Helen gasped. She ran towards the campsite until she had a clear view over the wall. She saw tents and bikes.

But no canoes.

The canoes were on the minibuses. The Scouts didn't have to come back here to go to sea. They could be launching from anywhere along the north coast. They could be in the sea already!

How could Helen find them to warn them? Sheila might know where they were planning to go. But Sheila had helped set this task up. Helen couldn't trust Sheila to tell the truth. She had to find them herself.

Helen thought about the coastline. There was a long sandy beach to the west of the campsite. They could launch canoes from there, and it would be a great place for a barbecue. She should try there first.

She'd have to go by boat. Could she row there in time to warn the Scouts, or would she arrive just in time to pull their bodies from the sea?

She sprinted towards the jetty. Then she heard a noise which usually made her feel safe. She heard hooves on the ground.

She looked over to her left. Yann was galloping to the jetty, followed by Catesby and Lavender. Rona wasn't with them. Was she still weeping in the tent? Or had she already left on her murderous mission?

Helen ran faster. But she couldn't outrace a centaur.

When Helen reached the wooden jetty, still slippy from the morning's rain, Yann was there before her. Standing on the planks. Blocking her way to the boat.

"Let me past, Yann."

"No, I won't let you past. Listen to me ..."

"There's no time to listen. I have to save the Scouts."

"Helen, you don't understand ..." Yann's voice rose above Lavender's high-pitched arguments and Catesby's insistent chattering, as the fairy and the phoenix circled Helen and fought for her attention. But they couldn't stop her getting in the boat. Only Yann could stop her. So she concentrated on him.

"I don't understand why you aren't trying to save them, Yann! Are all you fabled beasts the same? Killing people for sport?" She was shouting over his protests. "Do you all think of humans as enemies, or prey, or pawns in your magical games? Why should I listen to you? You've never trusted humans, so maybe you've never trusted me!"

"Helen, that's not fair!"

"This isn't about fair. This is about lives. I'm going to stop this contest, I'm going to save those Scouts, and I'm going to make sure fabled beasts *never* hurt people again. I'm going to protect humans from what they don't yet know is there."

"Are you going to *tell* them?"

"If I have to!"

"Helen! You can't!"

"Yes, I can. And I will, if it saves the Scouts. Are you going to stop me?"

The two of them faced each other, Yann towering over her, his fighting face on, his fists clenched.

Helen knew how strong Yann was, how much he prided himself on his fighting skills. Would he hurt her, to stop her getting on the boat?

She'd accused him of not trusting her. She'd said she might betray his world.

But would he hurt her?

Helen realised she still trusted their friendship. So she stepped towards the boat.

Yann barged into her, using the weight of his horse body and the height of his horse shoulders to push her backwards.

"Yann!" she said indignantly. She stepped forward again.

He kicked the air, rearing up, his huge heavy hooves whistling past her head.

Helen jerked back, shocked.

"Yann! Your hooves nearly hit me!"

"They *will* hit you, human girl, if you try to get past me again," he said through gritted teeth. "Go back to the tent. Go back now."

Helen looked up at him, embarrassed to realise there were tears in her eyes. Yann had tried to kick her!

Even when they first met, even when he didn't like her or trust her, he had never tried to hurt her. Maybe nothing had changed. Maybe he still didn't like her or trust her. Maybe they were all using her, her music, her first aid skills, her connections to the human world.

Helen wasn't going to be used any more. She was making her own decisions now. She took another step forward.

Yann raised a hoof.

She looked down at his hooves. And she saw the messy coils of rope on the wet jetty. When they'd landed with the injured mermaid, Helen had been too rushed to tie up neatly.

She looked at the tangle of yellow rope. And at the four dark hooves.

Helen bit her lip. Did she really think she could beat Yann?

She stepped to the left, and Yann covered that move. She stepped to her right, and he moved too. His back left hoof stepped into a loop of rope.

Helen looked around the jetty, as if looking for an escape route, but really hoping to distract him from the rope at his hooves. Just behind her, she saw something to distract him even more.

A long stick with a hook, like the pole her teacher used to open high windows in the classroom. She'd seen Sheila use this to haul waterlogged ropes out of the harbour. She grabbed it and waved the hooked end at Yann.

"Helen!" he said in exasperation. "Don't take up weapons against me!"

"Why not?"

"Because you're my friend. Because I don't want to hurt you." His voice was cracking. "But I can't let you betray the selkies, or our whole world. Please put that down. I don't want to hurt you, Helen."

Helen jabbed the hooked pole at his chest.

He sidestepped the attack. Now two hooves were inside circles of rope.

"You know I have never been defeated. Not by anyone less than twice my size."

"Then it's high time you *were* defeated, you arrogant centaur."

She swung the weapon at him. He stepped back to avoid the hook.

"Helen! Don't do that!"

He stepped forward again, his front hooves placed into another rope tangle.

Lavender was shouting and Catesby was squawking, and Helen swung the pole again.

The centaur sighed. His hand flicked out, grabbed the pole, pulled it out of her hands, and threw it into the sea.

He crossed his arms and grinned. "Right. Enough of that foolishness. Let's go back to the tent and talk about this sensibly. You need to know ..."

"I already know everything I need to. Including what you're standing in."

He looked down. She darted forward and pulled the rope. It tightened round his hooves and fetlocks. He kicked out but nearly lost his balance.

For the first time, Yann was as angry as Helen. He yelled, "Don't you dare!" Lavender and Catesby were swooping at her, shrieking and pulling her hair.

She hauled on the rope again. Yann kicked out once more, and his right front hoof struck her thigh. His leg was hobbled by the rope, so the kick didn't quite knock Helen over. But it did force her back, limping and gasping with pain.

She looked down. The rope was still wrapped round Yann's hooves and legs, so she jerked the end as hard as she could. The centaur teetered on the slippy planks and fell backwards off the jetty, into the shallow water of the harbour.

Helen leapt into the boat, untied the tangled rope, and grabbed the oars.

As she rowed out to sea, facing the campsite, she watched a wet, angry, seaweed-covered centaur trying to clamber onto the jetty. She called, just loud enough for him to hear, "Who's one step ahead now?"

Chapter 20

Helen navigated herself towards the beach where she hoped she'd find the Scouts by keeping the constantly changing colours of the coastline's cliffs, hills and beaches on her right.

She had learnt to row on a loch, with no big waves and no sharp rocks, and she'd never been out at sea on her own. But the sea was calm, she stayed close to the shore, and the boat was lighter without Yann.

Without anyone else to keep a lookout, she had to twist round regularly to check what was in front of the boat. She avoided the rocks she could see, and hoped there weren't any submerged.

Then she heard her name being called. She looked up, and saw two bright dots against the pale cliffs. Catesby and Lavender.

The fairy screamed, "*Wait!* It's not ... The Scouts are ..." Every third or fourth word was lost in the noise of water and seabirds. Catesby was flying round Lavender, his beak protecting the tiny fairy from the razorbills and guillemots on the cliff face, his wings sheltering her from the air currents.

Helen sighed. They had chased her out to sea, where neither of them had the weight to resist any wind, all to help their friend Rona win.

"Helen, you might *drown!*" Lavender squealed.

Alright, maybe they were worried about her too. But they weren't even slightly worried about the Scouts.

So Helen ignored her friends, and kept rowing along the curved coastline. Next time she turned round, she saw two stacks, tall fingers of rock sticking out of the water, at the point of a long headland. She recognised the Old Man and the Old Woman of Skerness, and she knew the wide beach was just beyond them.

Suddenly she heard a sound which made her fingers tighten and her spine freeze. She heard a song. A song which *she* had written with Rona a few weeks ago.

Rona was storm singing.

So the Scouts, and the contestants trying to drown them, must be at the beach behind that headland. Helen had come to the right place. But she'd got here too late. The task had started.

She could hear Rona adjusting her beat and pace so the song spoke with the wind and waves.

Helen felt a surge under the boat. The waves were joining in! The song was working. She regretted every minute she'd spent on this song, and regretted even more giving Rona the idea of how to sing a storm.

She heard another faint line of song, from further away or in a weaker voice. Serena's voice? A song calling not to a storm, but to Helen's heart, calling her closer, to adore the singer.

Helen stopped rowing at the foot of the stacks. She'd just realised something really obvious, something which Lavender had been trying to tell her.

Helen was in a boat.

The storm which Rona was singing up, the magnetic song of the mermaid, whatever weapon Tangaroa would use to sink his canoes. These would all work on her and her boat too. How could she possibly save anyone else?

She considered her chances. This boat was bigger, heavier and more stable than a canoe. She knew she was in danger, which might make her harder for Serena to fool, and harder for Tangaroa to attack, though no less vulnerable to the weather called up by her best friend.

So she hauled on the oars again. Once she'd rowed past the Old Man's feet, she twisted round for a sudden open view of a bay filled with canoes, and a flat golden beach beyond. The wind was already whipping her hair around her face.

She glanced back the way she'd come. She couldn't see Catesby and Lavender. When she'd paid no attention, they must have given up.

There were almost twenty canoes paddling off the beach. It was too late to warn them all; she would have to save individual Scouts. She could see a jumble of rocks out to the west, where the mermaid's song was coming from, and a white vortex of spray in the open sea, which must be Rona's storm. Tangaroa could be under the water anywhere off the beach.

Helen started rowing for the heart of the storm. It was nearest to her, so she could reach it and those endangered Scouts fastest. Also, if she saved the Scouts in the storm, then she could prevent Rona becoming a killer. She wanted to do that for her friend, even if Rona wouldn't thank her.

The nearer she got to the canoes, the louder she could hear Serena's song.

"Come to me and sing with me,
Swim with me and sink with me."

Helen's arms kept trying to pull that way, to get nearer to the song, to learn it, to join in with it.

So Helen started to hum a piece of music she'd learnt last summer, music which battled against the mermaid's song in her ears and her mind, diluting its power. Now she could control her arms and the oars; now she could row towards the Storm Singer and her storm.

Within moments she was in a whirling confusion of weather. She couldn't hear the call of Serena's song; she could barely hear Rona's song. She was almost deafened by the whipping wind and crashing waves. The boat was harder to control, with water pouring over the bow and swirling in the bottom of the boat.

She twisted round to see how the lighter canoes were coping. There were about five or six trapped inside the selkie's storm.

She watched in horror as a yellow canoe flipped over, and a red one vanished under the waves. A blue canoe was thrown into the air, and fell back prow first into the sea, tipping the canoeist out. A green canoe bobbed past her, upside down.

Two orange canoes were pressed close together, holding each other steady. The storm intensified around those two canoes and their screaming occupants, trying to force them under. But after each huge wave hit them, they bounced back up, like rubber ducks in a bath. So Helen rowed past, heading for the sinking Scouts further on.

The waves made one more attempt to sink the orange canoes, and hit Helen's boat on the way past, stinging her eyes, almost pulling the oars out of her hands.

As she rowed on, she saw long clear tentacles wrapped round the prows of the orange canoes, pushing them up out of the attacking waves.

Helen blinked her sore eyes. Was that the sea-through? Saving the Scouts? Why would it do that?

She reached the nearest splashing Scout. It was Emily, who'd been so scathing about Lavender's dresses. Helen almost screamed in frustration as she tried to keep the boat steady and haul the soaking weight of a girl much bigger than her into the boat. Emily managed to hook her own arms then legs over, and clambered in.

Helen rowed to the next Scout in the waves. She controlled the boat while Emily pulled the boy out of the water.

Then Helen noticed the song had stopped, the waves and wind were dying down, her boat was easier to control.

As the spray left the air, she saw a dark head bobbing in the water.

Rona was beside the red canoe, her pale human arms reaching out for it.

Helen wondered if Rona was planning to pull people

under the water personally, rather than let the wind and waves do it for her, and she started to row frantically towards the selkie and her victim.

But Rona rolled the canoe upright, then patted the canoeist, who was still inside, on the back to get water out of her mouth.

Helen called out, "Are you having a change of heart, killer?"

Rona swam over to the rowing boat, and glanced at the two Scouts, too busy spluttering to notice her. "No, Helen, I've not had a change of heart, I'm still trying to *win*!"

"What?"

"I don't win by drowning them, you silly fool. I win by *saving them*." She swam off towards the next struggling swimmer.

Helen stood up, rocking the boat in the choppy sea, and saw Rona guide another canoeist back to his boat, keeping his head above water.

Helen frowned. She turned towards Serena's rocks. There was a confused-looking canoeist paddling in a circle, several broken and holed canoes floating nearby, and a group of bedraggled canoeists perched on the rocks. Serena, standing on her skinny legs, was pulling one last Scout out of the water.

At the beach, Helen recognised Tangaroa, his blue tattoos covered with a wetsuit, hauling a limp canoeist up the sand.

Helen sat down again, sighed deeply, and looked at the two Scouts she'd saved. "I'd better get you to shore."

The beach was chaos: coughing Scouts, shouting leaders, boats being sent to fetch the Scouts on the rocks, heads being counted and hot drinks being made. So no one asked Helen any awkward questions. She helped the two Scouts onto the sand, and rowed away as fast as she could.

Once she was round the headland, she stopped rowing, and let the boat drift, shivering and rubbing tears from her eyes.

Five minutes later, a dark head popped up beside the boat, and Rona climbed in. She sat at the stern, smoothing down her grey dress, and holding her wet skin in one hand.

After a moment, Rona said, "They're all fine. All safe on the beach. A few canoes are wrecked, but that's a risk they take when they go to sea."

Helen was silent, not sure if she should apologise or continue the argument she'd walked out on earlier.

Rona was happy with silence. She wasn't a chatterer like Lavender. She sat calmly, folding her skin neatly, brushing the fur the right way.

Helen wanted to break the silence, but she had no idea what to say.

Rona stood up, stepped lightly to the middle bench, and put her arms round Helen. "I'm sorry."

"What are you sorry for? I'm the one who didn't trust my friends, stomped off in a tantrum, then ruined your contest. Did you win?"

"No."

"Why not? You sang up a lovely storm."

"I didn't sink two of my boats. And I didn't save everyone who went in."

"I thought you said they were all fine?"

"They are. But you saved two of mine, so I don't get points for them."

"Sorry. Were the orange ones the two that didn't sink?"

"Yes. No matter how high I made the waves, I just couldn't push them under. I had to stop trying so I could save the four already in the water. So I'd no chance of winning. Even before you interfered."

"I'm sorry. But I'm also confused. Was the task to sink them *and* to rescue them?"

"Of course," said Rona. "Why wouldn't it be? Selkies and mermaids often rescue sailors, you must have heard the old stories ..."

"But surely you don't want *new* stories, about selkies and mermaids spotted on the coast *now*. Didn't they see you?"

"They saw us, but we can all look human, so they don't know what saved them."

"Or what sank them," said Helen. "None of them did drown, but some of them might have if you hadn't got to them on time. It was really dangerous!"

"No, it wasn't! Every single adult selkie, mermaid and blue man was in that bay, ready to swim to the Scouts' aid. If the contestants hadn't saved them, not one of them would have drowned. They were safer this afternoon than any time they've ever been out in their canoes."

"They didn't know that. Neither did I."

"You didn't let me tell you. You wouldn't listen when I tried to explain."

"If you'd told me about the second task the first time I asked, rather than letting Serena put the worst possible spin on it ..."

"I didn't think you'd approve of us scaring them like that," Rona said, quietly.

"I don't, but scaring isn't as bad as killing."

"I can't believe you thought I'd drown them!"

"I'm sorry I didn't trust you."

Rona was quiet, stroking her damp fur again, like a pet on her knee.

"So who did win?" Helen asked eventually.

"Tangaroa. He got six and six. Serena only smashed five of her six on the rocks because one of them had headphones in and didn't hear her song properly. I was last: I only sank four and only saved *two*! But there are no prizes for second or third, so that's one task to me, one to Tangaroa and nothing to Serena so far."

Helen remembered something. "Those orange canoes. They didn't sink because they were being held up by the sea-through."

"Really?" Rona stood up and looked round. "Why would a sea-through save humans? They're usually angry when humans trespass on the sea."

"Maybe it cares more about stopping you winning than about stopping trespassers. Maybe that's its plan. Rona, I really need to tell you what Lavender and I heard the sea-through say last night ..."

"You saw the sea-through last night?"

"Yes, but first, I'd better apologise to Yann."

"Why?"

"After you left, I had an argument with him too. A fight, really."

"You had a *fight* with Yann? With fists and everything?"

"Not fists, just sticks and hooves and stuff."

"Helen, are you alright?"

"I'm fine. I won."

"You *won*! You beat Yann in a fight?"

"Yes."

"*How?*"

"I tangled his hooves up in a rope, pulled the end and he fell in the bay."

Rona's face was a mix of admiration, shock and fear. "Wow. Are you sure you want to apologise? Wouldn't you be safer staying out here, at sea, until he calms down? You can stay with me for months, years, forever, if you need to ..."

"Thanks, but I'd better say sorry. Is he still at the campsite?"

"No," said Rona, "he's there." She pointed inland, to the tall centaur standing on the shore, as still and solid as the stacks of Skerness. "Do you want me to come with you? Stand between you?"

"To protect me? No, it's ok. You need to get ready for the next task."

Rona smiled in relief. "You're sure? Good luck then. I'll see you back at the campsite. You can tell me about the sea-through, and we can have a chat about tomorrow's quest. I'll need Lavender's wisdom and Yann's fighting tactics. Maybe I should ask you for battle tips too, my warrior friend!" She gave Helen a hug, and dived off the boat.

Helen rowed to shore, almost as nervous about facing Yann now as she had been on the jetty.

Yann didn't say anything as she approached. He just stared out to sea.

She climbed out and stood beside him. He didn't look at her.

Helen realised she didn't want to apologise to him. She had beaten him fair and square, and didn't see why she should be ashamed of that.

"Tangaroa won," she said, keeping her voice steady. "And all the Scouts are safe."

"All the Scouts are safe. What a surprise. To you, but not to anyone else." His voice was hard and chilly.

"I'm not going to say sorry," Helen said firmly. "Not for getting you wet."

He didn't answer.

"I did say sorry to Rona, for thinking she wanted to drown people. So I should probably say sorry for thinking you would help her, for thinking you would stop me saving lives. So I am sorry. But not for beating you in a fight."

"You're not sorry?" Yann said, slowly.

Helen shook her head. "Not sorry at all."

She sneaked a sideways glance at him, but he was still staring out to sea.

"Then I'm not going to apologise either. Not for trying to stop you making a fool of yourself, nor for trying to stop you disrupting Rona's task."

There was silence.

"I can't believe you fought back," he said quietly. "That was so reckless."

She didn't answer. He was right. It had been really daft.

"It was an excellent fight though." Yann's voice was a little warmer. "You had some good moves. For someone so small and weak and untrained."

"I was angry. And scared."

"Scared? Of me?"

"I'm not sure. Scared of everything. Of the Scouts drowning. Of this whole magical world. Of your hooves. Particularly your hooves."

"I kicked you, didn't I? Are you hurt?"

"Yeah. I've got a big bruise on my leg."

She looked at him again. He was staring at her now, frowning.

She rubbed her leg and winced. "But I think I got off lightly, for someone who fought a centaur. I should have trusted you. I am sorry for that. I won't doubt my friends again, I promise. Do you forgive me?"

"Forgive you for what? For doubting Rona? For making her lose the task? For fighting me? For beating me? For *embarrassing me*?" he roared at the top of his voice, and Helen had to make an effort not to step away from him.

"Em. Yes. For all of that. Do you forgive me?"

"Of course. You were doing what you believed was right, even though it was wrong. And you were much better at fighting than I expected, which is yet another reason for me to be proud you're my friend. Of course I forgive you. Do you forgive me for kicking you?"

"Yes. And for being an arrogant idiot, who would rather fight than finish a sentence. If you had *told* me ..."

"If you had *listened* ..."

They stared at each other, and Yann laughed. He held out his hand. Helen smiled, and shook it. "Good," he said, "we don't even need a tug-of-war to make peace."

"Just as well," said Helen, "because you would definitely beat me at that!"

He laughed again. "Let's head back to Taltomie. Do you want a lift?"

"I'll have to row. I can't leave the boat here. And I need to apologise to Catesby and Lavender too when we get back, because I completely ignored them when they flew after me."

"Catesby and Lavender didn't go back to the campsite, not while I was on the way here," Yann said. "Aren't they with Rona?"

"No. The last time I saw them was at the cliffs, just before the storm started ... Yann! I haven't seen them since Rona sang up a storm!"

Yann was pale. "Neither have I!"

"Do you think they've been blown away?"

Yann looked out to sea again. "I hope not. I'll search along the shore, you search along the water's edge, and we'll both head for the campsite as fast as we can. If they aren't there, we'll have to ask the selkies to search for them at sea ..."

He trotted off, looking anxiously at tussocks of grass, and Helen rowed away, checking the shallow water and the shoreline.

Then she found a single copper feather. The adult feather Catesby had been so proud of it. Floating on the surface of the sea. She picked it up, and rowed back to the campsite.

Chapter 21

"It's my fault! I sang up the weather," sobbed Rona.

"No, it's my fault! I wouldn't listen to them, so they kept following me," Helen sniffed.

Helen and Rona were sitting beside each other, looking at the feather on Helen's lap, tears running down their cheeks.

"It's not *anyone's* fault!" yelled Yann. "Or even if it is, sitting here *crying* about it won't help. We have to get out there and find them." Yann hustled the girls out of the tent into the evening sunshine.

Aunt Sheila, who hadn't looked Helen in the eye since they got back, had used her influence as a selkie elder to organise search parties of mermaids and blue loons out at sea, and selkies in human form along the shoreline.

Yann watched the sea tribes searching for his missing

friends. "They know the shore better than Helen and I do. We should leave them to it."

"So what can we do?" asked Helen, trying not to use her hankie when Yann was looking.

"We can think about what they would have done if the storm did catch them."

"Catesby was protecting Lavender from the seabirds and the wind," said Helen. "He would have kept her safe, unless the winds separated them."

"The winds which I sang up!" Rona started wailing again until she saw Yann's face. "Sorry. I'll concentrate."

"So would Lavender cling to Catesby's feathers, or would he use his beak to grab her clothes?" Yann asked. "How would that affect their aerodynamics and flight pattern?"

"I have no idea," said Helen. "They were sticking close to the cliffs, so if the winds were blowing away from Rona, they might have been carried inland rather than out to sea."

Rona sighed. "The air was swirling all over the place, especially when I was trying to sink those orange canoes. It's just as likely that they were blown out to sea ... oh dear ... Lavender *hates* getting wet!"

"Lavender just whinges about her clothes," said Yann. "She's really very tough. She'll be fine."

Yann was interrupted by a clanging from Sheila's house.

"Does that mean the searchers have found them?" asked Helen.

"No. It's a warning bell. The Scouts must be coming back," gasped Rona. "The searchers have to get out of sight. We'll never find them now!"

176

Yann ducked back into his tall tent, as the selkies in the distance slipped into their sealskins, and the mermaids and blue loons swam further out to sea. Helen and Rona watched three minibuses drive up.

"Will they recognise us?" Helen whispered.

"Of course. They saw us yesterday when we said we'd a burst pipe."

"No, I mean will they recognise us as the people who rescued them?"

"I doubt it," said Rona. "They were confused and their eyes were full of water."

They stood to one side, as the sodden Scouts clambered out of the minibuses. Helen saw several of them give Rona funny looks, and Emily started to walk towards them. Helen smiled calmly, as if nothing strange had been happening, so the Scout shook her head and went into her tent instead.

After a few minutes of milling around, the campsite was quiet again. All the Scouts were in their tents getting dry clothes, or in the toilet block having hot showers.

Then Helen heard a tiny sneeze, from the direction of the parked minibuses. She sprinted over. Where had that sneeze come from? She looked in the nearest door. The seats were all empty.

There was another sneeze from above her. She banged her head on the doorframe as she leapt back and looked up.

There, clinging to the roofrack, soaking wet and miserable, were Lavender and Catesby.

Lavender was so wet her dress was indigo. Catesby was a bony muddy brown.

Helen reached up and her friends fell into her arms.

She ran towards Yann's tent and stumbled in, followed by Rona.

"They're here, they're alive! And they're freezing! Hand me a towel, or that horse blanket if it's all you've got."

For a few moments no one spoke, as they carefully dried Lavender and Catesby. Then they started asking questions:

"Why were you on the minibus roof?"

"We were too tired to fly, so we hitched a lift from the beach, but that's not the important thing ..."

"Were you blown out to sea?"

"Yes, but that's not what we have to tell you ..."

"How did you get back to shore?"

"We used every bit of energy we had, so don't make us shout. Shut up and listen!"

Helen, Rona and Yann stopped asking questions, and Lavender, who hadn't complained once about her ruined dress, started to talk.

"We know why the sea-through has been attacking selkies. It wants to manipulate the Sea Herald contest to make its own favourite win! When we were blown over the water, we saw a massive colony of sea-throughs just under the surface, all joined together. That's a bloom, isn't it, Rona?"

"Yes," the selkie said faintly, her head in her hands.

"But it wasn't lots of individual sea-throughs in a shoal or a flock. They were linked together like one animal: all their tentacles on the outside, all their stomachs making one big pink intestine in the middle."

Catesby made a retching noise, and Lavender nodded. "It was pretty yucky, even though pink and purple usually go well together. When we were hovering above the bloom, trying to get our bearings, the big sea-through which attacked you swam back. We heard what it said, just before it sank itself into the bloom.

"It said, 'I hindered one to help another. Soon we will control the Sea Herald, then we will glory in a true equinox battle, and the sea will take back what belongs to the sea.' It chanted that last part, and the others in the bloom joined in. Then it squidged into the bloom, and the whole thing sank below the surface.

"So there's not just one sea-through, there's a huge slimy lump of them, and they're trying to control the contest, the herald and the ritual battle. Which is all very important, and helps explain what Helen and I heard on the beach last night, and we do need to talk about it, but could I put a dry dress on first?"

Lavender made herself a little changing room of darkness in the corner, as Helen quickly updated the two newcomers on how the sea-through had interfered with the second task, and how Tangaroa had won this round.

Rona wasn't really listening. She just shook her head. "A bloom. There hasn't been a bloom here for centuries. Blooms are obsessed with returning sea-grown or sea-drowned objects to the sea. If this bloom can turn the ritual fight into a true battle, that would certainly get some of the sea's possessions back."

"How?" asked Helen.

"A real battle between Merras and Thalas would produce waves and surges so high that water would flood at least a mile inland, dragging everything back out to sea, whether it used to belong to the sea or not.

The battle storm would also drown animals and people, flood caves, and, if our legends are true, crack cliffs, smash boulders into mountains, eat away at beaches and change the shape of the coast. That's why the Sea Heralds were created, to stop the real battles, to prevent destruction of the coast."

They all sat quietly, listening to the gentle murmur of the sea outside. Then Helen asked, "Should we tell your family?"

"Of course we should. The tribes can search for the bloom at sea, and the judges can watch out for the sea-through at the task tomorrow."

"Let's not tell them yet," said Lavender, emerging from her little shadow in a tidy blue dress. "We might need the judges off guard rather than on guard tomorrow. Let's think about this. Let's fit it together with what we overheard last night, which we haven't had a minute to discuss with Rona."

So Helen and Lavender explained how they'd followed the sea-through and what they'd heard on the beach.

"Who do you think the selkie was, Rona?" Lavender asked eagerly. "What do you think their failed plan was, and what do you think they're planning to do next?"

Rona looked overwhelmed by Lavender's questions. "Is one of my tribe a traitor? Working with the sea-through to destroy the coast? I can't believe that ..."

"Whoever the selkie was," said Helen, "he wanted a crown. Rona, does that sound familiar?"

"That must be the lost crown of the selkies!" whispered Rona. "We've not had a king for generations. Each colony governs itself now, and the crown has been hidden, so no one is tempted to rule all the selkies at once. But there's one family on Eilan nan MacCodrum which traces its line back to the ancient kings, one selkie family who love to boast about their royal blood. I wonder ... Surely not ..." She drifted off into silence.

Helen said suddenly, "Roxburgh sang about his royal ancestors at the Storm Singing competition yesterday. Is that who you mean, Rona?"

She nodded sadly. "On his father's side, Roxy's family claim direct descent from the selkie kings."

Catesby squawked a question.

Lavender answered, "No, it wasn't Roxburgh meeting the sea-through last night. It was a fully grown selkie."

Helen remembered the moment when she thought she'd recognised the voice. The selkie on the beach blustering: *But, but, but ...*

"Sinclair!" she blurted out. "It was Sinclair! He sounded just like that on the clifftop, when Strathy insisted Rona was still the winner."

"That doesn't make any sense," said Rona. "The sea-through attacked Roxburgh and tried to stop him winning, so why would Sinclair work *with* the sea-through?"

Yann shook his head. "Perhaps the sea-through wasn't attacking Roxburgh to stop him winning. You even said, Helen, that Roxburgh impressed the audience by singing brilliantly despite the distraction, so if Rona hadn't actually sung up a storm, Roxburgh would have won. Perhaps the sea-through wasn't sabotaging him. Perhaps the sea-through was *helping him*. Perhaps it was making him look like a true Storm Singer, by singing through an attack, just like Strathy said."

Lavender whirled round with excitement. "Yes!

181

Maybe that's the plan which failed yesterday! Maybe the sea-through wanted Roxburgh to become Storm Singer, so he would be the selkie participant in the Sea Herald contest, then win that too. That's why the sea-through doesn't think Sinclair can help any more, because Roxburgh can't become Sea Herald."

Yann nodded. "We should talk to Roxburgh. Find out if he did expect that attack, if that's why he was able to sing through it. And ask what the sea-through wanted him to do if he won."

"What if he won't answer?" Helen asked.

Yann lifted his hoof, and stamped it down. "I'm looking for a fight I can win today. I'll make sure he answers."

Chapter 22

Helen sighed. "Do I have to row along the coast again, hunting for Roxburgh?"

Rona shook her head. "We can walk to Roxy's favourite hangout. He'll be on the pebble beach, with the selkie boys from other colonies here to watch the contest."

Yann said, "We need to speak to him privately, so we'd better get the search for Lavender and Catesby called off."

Lavender nodded. "Catesby, please fly to Sheila's, and say we're both safe, but don't mention the bloom. Not yet. We need to hear Roxburgh's story before we decide who to trust."

So Catesby flew towards the house, as the others walked round to the shore. At the beach, they found a group of teenage selkies skimming stones, so Helen, Rona and Lavender headed towards the boys.

"Roxburgh," shouted Rona. "Can we have a word?"

"Oooh!" called his mates. "The ladies want a word, Roxy!"

Roxburgh blushed, and his mates pushed him forward, then dived into the water and swam offshore, sniggering.

Helen pointed the way round a large boulder.

Where Roxburgh walked right into Yann.

Roxburgh immediately backed off. But Helen and Rona blocked his way, and Lavender pointed her wand at him.

"Don't rush off, Roxburgh," said Yann. "We have a few questions. Why did the sea-through try to help you win the Storm Singer competition?"

"It didn't! It was trying to ruin my song!"

"No, it wasn't," Helen said. "You were waiting for it to attack. I could hear you saving your voice's strength, to sing at your best once it attacked, to impress the audience."

Roxburgh shook his head.

Lavender said, "There's no point denying it. We heard your dad here last night, bargaining with the sea-through for the crown."

Roxburgh went pale, but still didn't say anything.

Yann stepped closer to the selkie. "If you'd rather answer these questions in front of Strathy and the other elders, we're happy to arrange that."

Roxburgh looked around frantically.

Yann said calmly, "The elders aren't here. Your father's not here either. You have to make this decision yourself. Tell us about the sea-through."

Roxburgh put his head in his hands and mumbled, "You're right. I *was* expecting the attack. The sea-through and my father had a deal to make me Storm Singer, then Sea Herald. My father didn't think I could beat Rona without help, so the sea-through offered a way for me to look brave as well as sound good, so they'd all vote for me. And if I needed help to win the Sea Herald contest I would get that too. Once I was herald, all I had to do was deliver a message written by the sea-through, rather than the message written by Thalas, and the sea-through would give my father what he's always wanted."

"The crown?" asked Helen.

He nodded. "My father has always wanted to be king. The sea-through said the collective memory of the bloom could find the lost selkie crown, and father could use the crown to rule all selkies, if I would deliver their message.

"I did want to be Storm Singer, and I do want my father to be king because then I'd be king next, and father never gives me a choice anyway, so I agreed. But now I haven't won, I'm glad the plan failed. It would be pretty scary delivering the wrong message to Merras!"

"Who does the sea-through want to win now?" asked Lavender.

"Anyone who's desperate for something the bloom can provide, I suppose." He turned to Rona. "But it doesn't want you, I do know that, so it would be safer for you to give up now ..." Then he shivered, and looked up at Yann. "Are you going to tell anyone?"

"Not now. Later, once we've worked out what's going on, you might need to tell the elders this story. Once they know, Roxburgh, you'll not have to worry about your father bossing you around any more."

The selkie boy looked both shocked and relieved. Suddenly Catesby swooped overhead, squawking softly.

Yann nodded to Roxburgh. "Thanks. If you think of anything else we need to know to get the sea-through and your father off your back, please tell us."

"I'm not on your side!"

Rona moved to let him past. "Once you know what the bloom wants to do, Roxburgh, you will be on our side."

When they were back in the tent, Yann muttered to Rona, "You're a lot braver than that little water rat …"

Lavender spoke over him, asking Catesby urgently, "Did you say the elders and judges are meeting in Sheila's kitchen?"

The phoenix nodded.

"Let's go and tell them right now," said Rona.

"Not yet," said Lavender. "We need to think this through. We know the sea-through is trying to fix the result of the Sea Herald contest, but now that Roxburgh can't win, who is the sea-through helping?"

Lavender started to answer her own question, hovering in the centre of the tent, counting facts on her fingers. "We know it doesn't want Rona to win. That's why it held her out of the tidal race, and probably why it tried to drown Helen, because if she'd drowned, you'd have been too upset to compete, wouldn't you?" Rona nodded, and squeezed Helen's hand.

"So does it want the blue loon to win?" Yann asked. "Is Tangaroa a traitor, like Sinclair?"

"He could be, but so could Serena," said Lavender.

"The sea-through hasn't helped her," Helen objected.

"It could have done. Today, at the beach, by holding up Rona's canoes, it ensured Rona would lose, which could just as easily have helped Serena win as Tangaroa."

"Maybe it doesn't mind which of them wins," said Helen. "Roxburgh said it could be anyone who wants something the bloom can find. The others both want to be Sea Herald to get something else: directions home, or lifting the curse. If the bloom has a long memory, it might be able to help either of them."

Lavender nodded vigorously. "So the sea-through doesn't mind whether Tangaroa or Serena wins, because it can bribe either of them. Therefore we have to make sure *neither* of them wins. We have to make sure Rona wins. Because what's the thing you've always wanted most in the world?"

"To be Storm Singer."

"You already have that. So you're the only contestant the bloom can't bribe. Which means you have to win, so the bloom can't control the herald or the battle, so the coastline will be safe."

"How can we make sure she wins?" asked Helen.

Lavender turned to Rona. "Tell us exactly what you have to do tomorrow."

"This last task is the quest to find the herald's holder. There are three holders in three different places, one for each contestant. Each quest starts with a riddle, which gives the location of a map. But the map has a guardian, who will fight to defend it. The contestant has to defeat the guardian, then follow the map to the holder. The first contestant to bring their holder home wins."

"How do you think you'll do?" asked Lavender. "And how will the other contestants do?"

"I might not solve a riddle as quickly as the verse-covered blue loon, but I'm sure I'll get it fairly fast. I'll be faster than the others at map reading and the race back, because Tangaroa prefers word trails to drawn maps, and Serena's tail injury will slow her down.

"But I'm nervous about the map guardian. We don't find out what kind of creature the guardian is until we get there. It could be *anything*. I'm worried I might just give up when I see the guardian, if it's big, or scary, or ..."

Lavender said insistently, "How will the others do against their map guardians?"

Rona shrugged, trying to wipe tears from her eyes. Helen, who never understood why selkies made dresses without pockets, dug a hanky out of her jeans, and shoved it at Rona.

Lavender turned to the centaur. "Yann, how will they do in a fight?"

"Tangaroa made peace rather than fight me at the feast, but I think that was good sense not cowardice. He's strong and ruthless, so I'm sure he'll beat his guardian without much trouble. I don't know about Serena. She could be vicious under all those simpers, though perhaps only when she's got friends to back her up. The sea-through could be that friend ..."

Yann stepped closer to Rona. "So for you to have a chance of finishing your quest before either of them, Rona, we need to work out how you can defeat the guardian."

"No," said Lavender, "it's simpler than that. For you to win, we need to *help* you defeat the guardian."

"Actually *help* me?" Rona was shocked out of her silence. "Actually fight it with me?"

"Yes."

"That's cheating! I'm meant to do it on my own."

"You would do it on your own if this was just about you winning a title. But this is about preserving the balance between land and sea and about saving lives. We have to help."

Yann interrupted, "Lavender, this is wrong. Rona can't cheat. We can't cheat. This is an ancient, honourable contest. We can't ruin it."

"Why not? Roxburgh and his dad cheated. Tangaroa may have been conspiring with the sea-through today. Serena might be waiting for help tomorrow."

"So if Rona is the only honest contestant, then let her stay that way."

"Don't be daft, Yann! As the only honest contestant, she'll *lose*!"

Yann shook his head. "It's better to lose honestly, than win dishonestly."

"Don't be such a prat, Yann," said Helen. "Most of the people in Sutherland and Caithness live by the sea. If a battle forces flood waters a mile inland, think of all the villages and towns which will be destroyed. And what if the battle moves around? Then coastlines everywhere will be hit. This battle could destroy hundreds, thousands of villages, towns and cities. We have a chance to stop that destruction before it starts.

"This isn't about honour or honesty, Yann. It's about survival. Anyway, it isn't what you think that matters. Rona, what do *you* think? Will you accept our help to win? Will you cheat?"

Chapter 23

They all stared at the selkie. She shivered. "I don't care about winning the contest. I don't want to be Sea Herald. But I don't want caves flooded, cliffs ripped down and lots of humans drowned. What belongs to the sea and what belongs to the land meet at the coast; the sea can't have it all. We have to defend our coastline, even if it means cheating."

"Why not just tell the elders?" pleaded Yann. "Then you wouldn't have to cheat, they could stop the sea-through and bloom interfering, they could make sure the winning Sea Herald is honest."

Lavender laughed. "What? The mighty quest warrior Yann Smith wants to let the *grown-ups* sort it out!"

Helen said more soothingly, "Yann, we know Sinclair

is conspiring with the sea-through, so we don't know if we can trust the other elders."

"Anyway," said Rona, "a bloom isn't easy to defeat. A girl and a centaur can defeat one sea-through, but it would take several sea tribes to deal with a large bloom. There may not be time to defeat it that way."

Catesby squawked at Yann's face, and Yann whacked him out of the way. "No! I am not trying to get out of a fight!" The centaur whirled away, and took a couple of deep breaths. Then he turned back with a grim smile. "Accusing me of being a coward won't turn me into a cheat."

"Yann, we can't do this without you," said Lavender. "Despite Helen's display this afternoon, you're our fighter. Whatever that guardian is, we need you. You wouldn't just be fighting for Rona, you'd be fighting for the miles of coastline that would be sucked under in a sea battle. Really ..." the fairy winked at Helen as she flitted in front of the centaur, "... really, it's your *duty* to fight for her, for your friends, for your whole country. Like going to war ..."

"War? Duty?" Yann shook his head. "You think of me as your warrior, your muscles, your fast transport, but apparently you also think I'm stupid. You think if you call me a coward I'll do anything daft to disprove it. Or if you dangle a war in front of me I'll leap into action. I'm not that easy to manipulate. I know what's right and what's wrong. This is *wrong*."

"Fine." Helen stood up. "If you prefer your code of honour to fighting baddies and saving the world, then we'll do it without you. But we have to start now."

"Why now?" asked Rona quietly.

"We need to steal the riddles now."

191

"Why? I know you're good at riddles, Helen, but I can solve it myself tomorrow."

"Solving it tomorrow is too late. We need to know the map location now, because we have to be hidden there before the judges and the guardian arrive. We can't just trot along behind you tomorrow. The judges are in Sheila's kitchen, so let's go and eavesdrop."

"That *really* feels like cheating," said Rona doubtfully.

"It is," snorted Yann, as the others left the tent. "It is cheating, and you'll regret it."

It was just as well they didn't have Yann with them, Helen thought as they crept up to the kitchen window, because centaurs aren't great at sneaking.

They heard a selkie voice say, "Are the guardians in place?"

Another voice said, "Not yet. They have been paid, though, and have agreed to be in place before dawn. They were amused when I added the danger money in case they got hurt, and I'm not convinced they listened when I reminded them they were not to *kill* the contestants."

Rona was shivering, and Helen slid her arm round her friend's shoulders. Helen wasn't feeling much better, because she'd just talked herself into fighting a creature which laughed at danger money and ignored health and safety instructions.

The first voice asked, "Do we have the final riddles yet?"

Another voice said, "Let me read out what I've written."

The eavesdroppers huddled closer, Lavender whispering, "Remember every word."

They heard paper rustle, then a voice spoke clearly:

"At my front pigeons coo,
At my middle water flows through,
At my top, cows go moo,
So the answer is ..."

"No, that's not correct," said a new voice. "Sheep graze above, not cows."

"But sheep don't moo, and I need an 'oo' rhyme."

Various voices chipped in with "boo?" and "loo?"

"The rhymes are too easy," said the first voice, which Helen now recognised as Strathy's. "We need something more cryptic, maybe about 'that which made me still falling through me'."

Another voice growled, "We don't want to make them too hard, and anyway, the use of 'through' is clever because it does not look like a rhyme. If we write it down, it might take her a while to realise the words do all rhyme."

"That's an idea," said the riddler. "We can confuse it with other 'oo' sounds, but different spellings. Like true, blue, glue, shoe, who ..."

"How are we doing with the other two?" Strathy asked.

"'Two' rhymes as well."

"We have enough 'oo's now. How is the lad's one coming along?"

"I've got:

"Once houses, now heather,
Once byres, now grass,
Once full of talk, now silent.
Is that clear? Or was it cleared?"

"Is it too complex?" asked Strathy. "The 'clear' and 'cleared' is clever, but he's not local, will he know this area's history?"

"Oh yes," said a soft voice, "we had the same in the Western Isles. And we visited that village on the first day here, when you showed us the areas likely to attract human tourists. I'm sure he will get that."

"And the final one?"

"It's really elegant," the riddler said, proudly.

"Sky over you,
Surface over you,
Rock over you.
When the upside down you is over you,
Your search will be over."

"More puns," said Strathy. "Is it too simple?"

"If we read it out, so she hears the fourth 'you' rather than sees it, that might be confusing for a minute or two."

The elders agreed the final riddle, so Lavender gestured the friends silently back to the tent.

Yann was still sulking, so Lavender took charge, just like Strathy in the kitchen. "We don't have to solve the silence and cleared and village one, because it's for Tangaroa."

"No need to solve it, because it's so easy," laughed Helen. "The word 'cleared' and him knowing his history, it must be the Highland Clearances."

"And if tourists visit it, it must be the clearance village in Strathnaver," added Rona.

"The others aren't so easy," sighed Helen.

"Do the upside down one next," suggested Lavender.

"It should be a similar distance from here as Strathnaver, so that gives us a clue."

"Rock over you ...
Upside down you ..."

They all murmured the riddle to themselves.

"Upside down you, that doesn't make any sense, unless ..." Helen dipped a fingertip in the puddle of water which had dripped from Catesby's feathers, and drew a wet U on the groundsheet. "A letter U, look! If you turn it upside down ..." she drew again, "... it's an arch! With the sky, the rock and the surface over you ... Rona, is there an underwater arch nearby?"

"Yes, Fenia's Gateway. But," Rona's voice wobbled, "but how could you help me underwater?"

"Don't panic," said Lavender. "There's still one more riddle, the rhyming one." She repeated it out loud.

Rona snorted. "Pigeons cooing and cows mooing. It's like a nursery rhyme."

"They suggested another clue," Helen remembered. "'What made me still falls through me ...' What could that mean?"

They sat quietly for a while, with the occasional mutter of "moo", "loo", "blue" ...

Then Yann stamped his hoof. "It's so obvious! It's a cave! What made me, still falling through me, and water in the middle going through. Water, through rock, makes a cave!"

"Thanks for bothering to join in," snapped Lavender, "but there are lots of caves round here, so that doesn't actually help much."

Helen said, "The answer must be a rhyme. Go through the alphabet."

"Boo, coo, do ..." They muttered their way through the alphabet, until Rona said, "Queue, roo, Sue, oh! Soo, smoo!"

The others stared at her.

"Smoo! Smoo Cave has a waterfall through it, and grass above it, and there are even pigeons nesting on ledges at the front. Smoo Cave! But how do we know which is mine? Smoo Cave or Fenia's Gateway? And Smoo Cave ..." Her voice fell. "It's deep and dark and huge. And it's half watery and half dry ..."

"How deep is the water in the cave?" asked Helen.

"It's really deep under the waterfall, but it flows out as a shallow river, just centimetres deep in places."

"So this one *is* your riddle," said Helen. "If it's not deep water, then Serena can't swim, she'd have to walk. The judges didn't seem that bothered about your safety, but they did want the riddles to be equally difficult, so they must be trying to keep the quests fair. It wouldn't be fair to give a mermaid a quest on land, because her legs are wobbly and sore.

"So he gets the village, she gets the arch, you get the cave. Now we have to decide how we can help you in the cave."

"Not now," said Rona. "We need to eat and sleep first."

"No," said a voice behind them. "No food. No sleep. We must go now."

It was Yann. "We have to recce the battleground, and work out our tactics, before the guardian or the judge arrive."

They were all staring at him.

"You're coming with us?" said Rona.

"Of course I'm coming with you. Not because you've shamed me or teased me into it, but because I've realised it's not really cheating to break rules in a contest that's already broken wide open. Come on. Let's get to Smoo Cave."

Helen rubbed her aching arm muscles. "Do I have to row a whole horse around the coast again?"

"No, because the moored boat would give away our location," said Yann. "If we're going to cheat, we're going to get away with it. I'll get us there much faster. It's time I ran a race too, even if it's only against middle-aged judges who're probably still arguing about what rhymes with 'moo'."

Before Yann could rush them all out of the tent, Helen grabbed the packed lunches, which had been forgotten in the arguments after the race, so that Rona wouldn't be starving as well as scared.

Then, in a storm of speed, they galloped along cliffs, over moors, round kyles, through sea air and darkening night, towards Smoo Cave.

Chapter 24

They arrived at a clifftop carpark after midnight.

"We're definitely here before the judges," said Yann, slightly out of breath. "Let's go down and check out this cave."

"But the guardian might be here already," said Rona, shakily.

"Why?" asked Lavender. "It doesn't need to be here until dawn."

"Maybe it's the kind of monster which *enjoys* lurking in deep dark drippy caves all night."

Helen laughed. "Rona, *you* live in a cave. Don't start building this guardian up into something from a horror film. It's only a task, not a fight to the death." Then she remembered the voice in the kitchen saying the guardians hadn't listened when told not to kill the contestants.

"Helen, don't downplay this creature," said Yann, as they followed the tourist signs and Lavender's lightballs along steep steps down the cliff. "It's more dangerous to underestimate than overestimate an opponent. Let's assume it's nasty, violent and large, with an array of effective weapons, and prepare accordingly. If it's actually a bunny rabbit with a sharp stick, we can laugh at our over-preparation once we're safe. So think huge, dangerous, fast and predatory."

"You're not helping," muttered Helen. "Rona's very nervous. Stop using words like weapons and predatory, and stop sounding like this is fun!"

"Sorry," he murmured.

They reached the foot of the steps, at the end of a long, high inlet, and crossed a wooden bridge over a river flowing out of a black hole in the cliff.

"There are two caves," explained Rona. "The outer one is huge and mostly dry, the inner one is smaller and flooded, because the river running from the hills has broken through the roof. We'll have to check both."

Lavender whispered, "Should we use light in the cave?"

"I'm sure we're first here, but even so, keep light and talk to a minimum when we're inside," said Yann. "Let's go in, have a look round, come back out to discuss tactics, then Rona can head home and the rest of us will go back in and hide."

So with Lavender's lightballs looking unusually pale, they walked into Smoo Cave.

Rona led them past a wide pillar into a high arched cave. There was a big teardrop-shaped hole in the roof, with a few smaller holes at its tail, and when Helen stood under them, she could see through to the stars.

Yann paced out the cave, checking it was empty, then Rona led them along a wooden walkway, through a tunnel, to a platform at the entrance to the inner cave. They were battered by spray and noise from a waterfall plunging through the high roof into a dark pool.

Lavender encouraged her lightballs to swoop round the cave. The walls were wet from the constant spray, and the wide sheet of water looked cold and deep.

Helen knelt on the planks of the platform to see if there was anything visible under the water, but she couldn't see any shapes or movement.

Rona leant even closer to the dark choppy surface. She gasped, then turned and ran, not stopping until she was out in the clear night air.

They all ran after her, Yann bringing up the rear.

"What did you see?" asked Helen.

"Nothing! I didn't see anything! We couldn't really see anything in the shadows of the big cave, either. They could put the map anywhere: high on a ledge, or underwater in that black pool, or up on the roof where the river falls in, because selkie maps don't mind getting wet.

"And the guardian could be anywhere and anything. It could be a monster from inland, because they must be using a land beast in Strathnaver. Or it could be a monster from the darkness of the far ocean, in that deep pool. It could be *anything* and I won't know until it attacks and I don't think I can do this!"

She sat down on a rock, near where the narrow river met the sea, and tried to gulp back tears. Helen crouched beside her. "We'll be with you."

"But you can't be at the entrance or the judge outside will see you, so what if it jumps me when I walk in? And you can't be in the water, so what if it's swimming down in the dark?"

Rona was weeping now. "I wish I knew what it *was*, because at the moment it's everything scary and dangerous all mixed up together! You know I'm not as brave as all of you. Walking into a cave to meet a creature which could *eat* me, which could bite and swallow and digest me ... I just can't do it. It's my worst nightmare. I'm sorry. I can't."

Helen looked at Rona's rock, then at a much larger rock nearer the mouth of the inlet. "You don't have to go into the cave at all."

"Of course she does," said Yann briskly. "The judges weren't inside the wreck or the tidal race, but they were stationed outside. There will be a judge out here, so Rona has to go in, and she has to come out with the map."

"No, she doesn't. I'll go in," said Helen. "You all hide inside, but I'll hide *out here*, behind that big rock, and swap places with Rona before she goes in."

"But you don't look like Rona," objected Yann.

"You could," said Lavender. "If you wear one of Rona's dresses – and you would look much nicer in a dress than those jeans – and if we style your hair so it's long and straight ..."

"We don't need to style my hair. If I get it wet, the weight of it will make it hang down, and the water will make it shiny like Rona's."

"So, in a dress and wet hair, Helen could look like a selkie," said Lavender. "The light will be dim just after dawn, and the judge will be expecting Rona, so he or she won't be looking for a switch."

"But the guardian will tell the judges it was defeated by a human, a centaur, a fairy and a phoenix, rather than a selkie," said Rona miserably. "I *have* to go in."

"The two winged ones could be mistaken for the birds which live in the cave ..." said Yann, thinking out loud, "Helen will be dressed as a selkie, and if I attack from behind ... it won't know what hit it." He nodded. "That could work. We'll have to split up. Helen will stay out here tonight, and one of us should stay with her, in case the sea-through is still hunting for that coral necklace."

Catesby cooed reassuringly.

Helen smiled at the phoenix. "Thanks."

"Fine," said Yann. "Try not to be too obvious when you fly into the cave at dawn, Catesby. Lavender and I will hide in the shadows of the outer cave all night, and watch the guardian arrive. And tomorrow morning, Rona, once you've pretended to puzzle over the riddle, get here fast and haul out behind that rock, then Helen will appear and come into the cave. Once we've defeated the guardian, Helen will come back behind the rock and give the map to you. And off you go to win the quest. Simple."

"But Helen doesn't have a dress!" Rona wailed.

"Calm down!" said Yann. "Let's eat our very late lunch, then I'll take you back to Taltomie and you can give me a dress for Helen."

Once they'd eaten the slightly stale sandwiches, Yann and Rona headed up the steps and galloped off. Then Helen searched the shoreline. With the help of Lavender's light and Catesby's sharp eyes, she found a crusty old plastic bottle. She rinsed it as clean as she could, filled it with water, then balanced it behind the large rock.

Lavender sat on her knee. "Are you sure about this, Helen? Once you're in the cave, we'll only be able to help from the shadows. It's probably more dangerous than we were admitting to Rona."

"I'll be fine," said Helen. "Yann says it'll just be a bunny rabbit with a sharp stick."

Catesby laughed heartily, but Lavender made a face and flew to the cave to find a hidden perch. Helen said "night night" to Catesby, who was keeping watch on the hill behind her. As she dozed off, with her arms pulled out of her sleeves and wrapped around her chest inside her fleece, she hoped the guardian wasn't pink and purple with tentacles.

She was woken by a soft touch on her face. Yann was standing above her, lit by a sprinkling of stars, holding out a dark green dress. "Rona says she's got another like this, which she'll wear for the quest." He paused. "Don't worry about tomorrow, Helen. I'll be right beside you. Just concentrate on the map, and I'll deal with the guardian."

"Thanks, Yann." He disappeared into the cave.

Helen pulled on the soft silky dress, amazed at how warm it was. She didn't even need to put her fleece back on, so she made a pillow out of her jeans and fleece, and dozed more comfortably.

She was woken by a loud *SPLASH* from the cave. She peered out from behind the rock, and in the early morning light, she saw a high wave surfing along the river out of the cave, followed by a chorus of smaller ripples. Something had fallen into the pool. Or something had jumped. The guardian had arrived.

Before she could wonder what that wave meant about the size and nature of the guardian, she heard a smaller splash from the seaward side, and saw a blue man step out of the dark water in the inlet.

The judge had a large kelp bag on his back, and he pulled out a hammer and a wooden sign. He marched a few paces up towards the carpark, and hammered the sign into the path. Helen nodded. The sign must be to keep humans away. She heard the whirr of wings behind her, as Catesby took the chance to fly to the cave.

The blue man came back down, and pulled a roll of silvery parchment out of the bag. Then he walked cautiously into the cave. Even the judge was frightened of the guardian, Helen thought.

She heard the sound of hammering from deep inside the cave. When the judge came back out, she crossed her fingers, hoping he wouldn't sit too near her rock. He perched on the bridge over the peaty brown river, opened his bag again, and pulled out his breakfast.

Helen tried not to think about the guardian in the cave, distracting herself by wondering what guardians the blue loon and the mermaid would have to fight, and whether the sea-through would help either of them. But she kept hearing that splash echoing round her head, and wondering what size of guardian could have sent a wave so high down such a shallow river.

She heard another splash behind her, and nearly screamed. Then a gentle voice said, "Let's give you long straight selkie hair." The bottle of manky cold water was tipped over Helen's head.

She gasped, and turned round. Rona was standing behind her, in an identical green dress. The selkie whispered, "Thank you for doing this."

Helen gripped her friend's hands, stood up, and walked out from behind the rock.

Chapter 25

Helen walked towards the cave. She didn't turn to look at the judge on the bridge, like she was too focused to acknowledge him, but really not wanting him to see her face.

She walked in the high arched entrance. There was no one else there. Perhaps Lavender was still asleep. Perhaps Catesby hadn't got to the cave before the blue man came back down the steps. Perhaps Yann had decided cheating was too dishonourable after all, and gone home. Perhaps she was alone.

Then she heard Lavender whisper, "We're at your back."

She smiled and walked deeper into Smoo Cave.

The early sunlight was faint through the holes in the roof. Helen turned slowly round, looking at the cave's floor and walls, searching for the map, the guardian and her friends.

She saw orange and purple feathers hovering near the roof. But no sign of Yann. Perhaps he was better at sneaking than she thought.

Also no sign of a huge guardian. Nor a map hammered onto a wall. She heard a faint squawk. She looked up, and saw Catesby pointing with his beak at the walkway.

The map was in the waterfall cave. The guardian would be there too. So Yann must be there, on the platform, waiting for her.

Perhaps Yann had already dealt with the guardian, perhaps she could just walk in, get the map and walk out.

She marched along the walkway towards the waterfall cave, her face battered by freezing wet air, and her ears filled with an overwhelming roar. The guardian must be massive, she thought, to have made a louder noise than this when it arrived.

Then she was right inside the cave, the fierce white of the waterfall in the darkness ahead of her, and a few of Lavender's palest lightballs drifting behind her. Helen hoped the tall shape at the darkest part of the platform was Yann.

His welcome voice said, "Helen, stay there."

Then she saw the map: a square of silver, nailed to the wall to the right of the waterfall. There was a deep black pool between her and the map.

She stepped forward.

"No!" ordered Yann.

The waterfall seemed to move up rather than down as the water exploded out of the pool. When the fountain of spray fell back, Helen saw a column of green stone standing in the middle of the pool.

Then it moved slightly, a ripple up the column. It wasn't stone. It was a long neck and head, staring at her with flat cold eyes.

A snake? A worm?

It opened its mouth. It didn't have two snake fangs, it had rows of sharp teeth. The head shot forward.

Helen leapt back. The mouth snapped shut with a squelch, the head pulled back, and the neck slid under the waterfall.

Not a snake. Not a worm.

"An eel," said Helen. "A giant eel."

She had retreated further than she thought. She was almost back in the outer cave, her hands clinging to the railing of the walkway, with Yann at her back, Lavender and Catesby above her.

"A giant eel," she repeated. "Does it have a sharp stick, Yann?"

"It doesn't need one," he said loudly. "It has the pool. It just has to stay where it is, and we can't get the map."

Helen took a step forward, just far enough in to see the map, and the water between her and the map. She thought about the eel under the water. She nodded. "It doesn't have to fight. It just has to be there. Because what kind of idiot would swim across that pool?"

She reached her hand out to touch the wall of the cave. "Could I climb round?" But the rock was too wet to grip safely.

She looked at Catesby. He nodded and flew cautiously round the edge of the water. Yann's hands squeezed Helen's shoulders as he watched his friend above the eel's pool.

Catesby hovered in front of the map, and tugged at it with his claws and beak, but the silvery paper was too strong for him to rip, and the nail was hammered in too far for him to pull out.

He flew back, shaking his head.

"It needs hands," Lavender yelled over the noise. "I'll go."

Yann replied, "Don't be daft, you couldn't carry the map even if you could get it loose. It's ten times your size. If it needs hands, I'd better go."

"No, you won't," said Helen. "You're a huge target with far too many legs. The eel will make horsemeat out of you, then tell the judges that some horse boy tried to get the map. I have to go. I'm wearing selkie clothes, so I'm the only one who can be seen swimming that pool without exposing our cheating."

Yann looked miserable. "Helen! How can I let you do that? I said I'd deal with the guardian."

"You aren't dressed for it, Yann, so I'll have to go. I'll swim fast, and ... I'll come back faster!"

She couldn't think of anything cleverer than that. Swim fast and hope the monster under the water didn't notice. She gulped. How would it feel to be in the water and know those teeth were under you?

"Maybe I could ... em ... not swim in a straight line? Not do what it expects?"

"That's a good idea, but we can do better," called Yann. "We'll distract it: kick the water, drop in stones, disturb the pool in several places at once. Give it more than one target. Give you a chance."

He went to the outer cave to collect an armful of stones, happier now he had a plan. When he returned, Helen nodded at her friends, pulled herself onto the railing, and dived in.

The first thing she noticed was how warm the selkie's

dress made her feel. She knew the water was cold, because her hands and feet were freezing, but her body was cosy in the shimmering material.

However, the dress wouldn't guard against teeth, and there was something huge and slimy coiled underneath her, so she swam as fast as she could.

Over the constant thunder of the waterfall, she heard rocks hit the surface on the other side of the pool, and drumming as hooves kicked the water behind her.

Suddenly she was at the rock wall.

Helen was treading water, a stationary target, as she ripped the map from the nail. There was thrashing movement under the water now, as if the eel was confused, turning in circles, trying to decide what to attack.

Catesby squawked above her and reached out his claws to grab the map, so her hands were free to swim. Then she pushed away from the wall and swam for the platform, her arms slicing down in the water.

Rocks were flying through the air, splashing all over the pool, but Helen wondered how long it would take the eel to realise she was the only target moving *away* from the map's position. She swam as fast as she could.

Then she was punched in the belly by a huge fist. Or a car. Or a train.

She was lifted out of the water, high into the air, arms and legs dangling down.

Then she was flicked up and fell down past the eel's head, sinking deep into the pool. Helen watched, frozen in the cold water, as the eel's neck curved, its toothy mouth opened, and it dived down after her.

But the warmth of the dress woke her up enough to twist out of the way, and she was thrown sideways in the dark water by the force of the eel plunging past her. She scrambled into a messy breaststroke back to the surface and tried to work out which way the platform was.

There were splashes to her left, so she kicked off in that direction, her eyes full of water, her blood full of panic.

She felt a pain in her ankle, then a tug on her foot, but she kept kicking and the pressure fell away. She managed one more forward lunge. A hand grabbed her and dragged her out of the water. "That was incredible, my human friend," Yann gasped.

Helen waggled her left leg. The end of her leg felt very light. And very sore.

"My foot! I think it bit off my foot!" She couldn't look down.

Lavender said, "No, it just pulled off your shoe. You're fine."

Helen looked down. Her ankle was bleeding, her sock was ripped, but her foot was still there.

There was a cough from the pool and her trainer popped up to the surface. Pushed by ripples from the waterfall, it bobbed towards the platform. Catesby squawked and Lavender said, "Don't be rude. No one would eat your smelly feet either."

"Do you want that back?" Yann leaned forward to retrieve it.

Helen saw a glitter of slime on the velcro and toothmarks on the sole. "No, it's ok, I've got another pair and some wellies back at the tent."

She rubbed her eyes. "I'd better take the map to Rona."

She looked at the walkway shining in the glow from Lavender's lightballs, carefully placed so they cast shadows for Yann to hide in.

"Has it given up?"

"I don't know," said Yann. "But it's in the water, and you're on land, so I think you just need to run."

Helen stood up, took the map from Catesby and ran.

She felt the platform behind her shake. She turned to see the eel's huge muscled body crash onto the planks between her and the darkness hiding her friends. She suddenly remembered that eels can move house: they can go overland from one river to another. This eel could chase her all the way to the Borders! She stood and stared at it. The eel looked back at her, its eyes bored and flat. It lunged forward.

She swerved and sprinted away, limping in her one shoe and one sock, but there was a wet thud behind her. She whirled back, and the eel pitched forward, landing open-mouthed at her feet. Its head bounced once on the wood, then lay still.

Yann stepped into the light. "Once it was out of the water, I could finally deal with it."

Helen smiled. "You'd better find a hoof-shaped stone to explain the bruise on its neck, while I take the map to Rona."

She walked through the outer cave, running a hand down her wet hair to make it straight, but as she reached the pillar at the entrance, she was jerked to a stop.

She almost overbalanced because she couldn't move her feet. She put her hand out to stop herself falling, and felt something wet wrap round her right wrist.

A voice hissed from behind the pillar. "A nasty little human with a fishskin parchment. That belongs to the sea." The sea-through slid round, pulling itself closer with the tentacles wrapped round Helen's ankles and right wrist. "You got it by *cheating*, didn't you? The sea won't like that. So I'll have it back."

"No!" Helen kept her voice quiet so the judge on the bridge wouldn't hear her. "You're the cheat. Helping Tangaroa, stopping Rona. All we're doing is making it fair."

The map was in her left hand, and she held it away from the pillar, out into the new yellow sunlight, as if she was reading it, but really so the sea-through couldn't reach it without stepping into the judge's eyeline.

"Give me the map!"

"No," said Helen, feeling her skin burn at wrist and ankles, and hoping her friends had realised she was being attacked.

But Yann and the others were covering their tracks round the unconscious eel, and Rona must stay hidden if they were to fool the judge. Helen had to deal with this herself.

She had no weapons, but she did have one thing on her side. The sea-through's obsession with the sea's possessions.

"The map *is* going back to the sea," she said. "Rona will take it straight to the sea, look." She threw the map out of the cave towards the water.

The judge looked puzzled, but went back to eating his breakfast.

"But this ..." Helen pushed back the left sleeve of the selkie dress to show the bracelet she'd made from her broken necklace. "... this coral will *never* go back to the sea." She used her teeth to pull off the bracelet and held it high.

"I'll throw it onto a ledge, the pigeons will carry it inland, the magpies will decorate a nest with it, it will sit in a tree for centuries and the sea will *never* get it back."

The sea-through squealed, and pulled its tentacles off her wrist and ankles. It reached up for the orange bracelet, as Helen flicked it into the air behind her, further inside the cave.

The sea-through darted after the bracelet like a dog after a squirrel, and Helen ran outside, picked up the map, and fell behind the rock.

"The guardian was a giant eel," she gasped. "The sea-through is right behind me. You'll have to sprint so it can't follow you."

Rona nodded, pulled the map from Helen's hands, hauled herself out from behind the rock and slid into the water.

The judge watched Rona swim out of the inlet, then walked into the cave. Helen held her breath. What would he find? A centaur? A sea-through? A fairy? A phoenix?

But her friends and enemy must have had time to hide, because soon the judge sauntered back out, picked up his bag, then dived into the sea.

A couple of minutes later the sea-through stumbled out, clutching the coral to its chest, and splashed into the water. Helen hoped it wouldn't catch up with Rona.

Finally, Yann, Lavender and Catesby came out, blinking in the morning light.

"Where's the eel?" asked Helen.

Yann grinned. "It's still out cold, but it's back in the pool. The judge kicked it in, presumably so it wouldn't dry out."

"What if it wakes up in a bad mood, and eats a tourist?" Then Helen looked up the path. "That's probably why the judge left the sign."

They walked up the steps to a notice written in deep blue ink:

Don't go down to the cave today,
Or you'll get a big surprise.
Don't go down to the cave today,
Or you'd better go in disguise.
Don't go down to the cave today ...
Finish the rhyme in seven words or less, prize for best entry! (But PLEASE DON'T go down to the cave today, or we won't be responsible for your safety.)

Helen laughed, and started thinking of rhymes about the eel's cold eyes, as Yann took them home, at a canter rather than a gallop.

"Did you look at the map?" Lavender asked. "Do you know where Rona's going?"

"No, I didn't have time." Helen explained about the sea-through attacking her.

"Of course. I should have thought of that," said Lavender, annoyed with herself. "The sea-through couldn't help Tangaroa on a quest far inland, and there was no point helping Serena because if she wins the result would be a tie. I should have realised it would try to stop Rona again. I hope it's not caught up with her."

"She has a good headstart, and it didn't see the map so it doesn't know where she's going," said Yann. "She'll be fine. All she has to do is follow the map, get the holder and come home. She'll be quite safe ..."

Chapter 26

Rona swam northeast, still feeling guilty about letting Helen go into the cave for her. At least she was doing the last part of the quest herself, following the map to a wreck far off the coast.

She was sprinting at top speed because she'd no idea how well the others were doing. She'd pretended to work out her riddle, and dived off the start rock before either of the others, but they can't have been far behind, so they might have defeated their guardians and be on the way to their holders too.

Rona knew the cheating at the cave didn't guarantee she'd win; it just gave her a chance she wouldn't have had otherwise, because she could never have walked towards the guardian the way Helen had.

Rona smiled a wide seal smile. Helen thought she

was an ordinary human girl with extraordinary friends. But Rona knew Helen was the most amazing of them all: accepting their magic, understanding their fear of humans, generous with her music and medical skills, and taking risks to protect her friends and their world. Rona decided she would write a new song for Helen, not to win a competition, nor to sing up a storm, but just to say thank you.

She was near the wreck now. She lunged up to the surface, and breathed deep, taking as much oxygen as her tired body could store.

The map, which she'd memorised then ripped to pieces and fed to a shoal of herring so the sea-through couldn't find it and follow her, hadn't shown her what the herald's holder actually was. She had to work that out for herself when she got to the wreck. Another riddle.

She breathed out, closed her nostrils, and dived.

Below her, she saw an unnatural shape on the seabed.

A wreck. But not a shipwreck.

A plane. Like a bird's shadow, but with one wing broken off.

She'd seen fighter planes and bombers on military exercises above Cape Wrath, confident no one lived there, not realising how close their bullets and bombs were to selkie colonies and pups.

This wasn't a fighter plane. It was far too big. As she got closer, she saw a huge hinged door at the back. It was some kind of cargo plane. It might be filled with all the goods it had been carrying. Her fur bristled as she realised it might even be filled with the people who had been flying it.

She reached the massive back door.

She twitched her whiskers nervously, reminded herself that she'd been a wimp at Smoo Cave in order to save her bravery for here, and swam into the plane.

It was empty. No bombs or crates of food or drowned human beings. Just a vast water-filled tube of metal. Every surface was encrusted with the growths which move in when something from land or air falls into water. The wreck must have been here since one of the human wars which brought so many soldiers and sinkings to the north coast.

Rona swam up the left side of the plane, seeing nothing which could hold a message. She flicked herself through a swinging door at the front end of the plane, into a small room filled with seats, levers, wheels and a wide glass window looking out at the darkened sea.

This must be where the humans sat to fly the plane. There were a couple of metal boxes, open and rusting, and a leather satchel hanging on the back of one of the webbing chairs. Rona flapped the bag open. Inside was a book, so waterlogged that when she pulled it out the pages fell apart, a handful of old metal-nibbed pens, and a glass bottle with a ceramic stopper.

A bottle.

Rona laughed.

A message in a bottle. It was the perfect holder.

She grasped the bottle awkwardly under her fin, then had a better idea. She put it back in the satchel, which she slipped onto her back, then turned to leave the plane.

She swam into the empty cargo space. Then stopped. And reversed very fast into the flying room at the front.

Of course. There had been a guardian for the map. There was a guardian for the holder too.

Rona poked her head round again.

The view was still the same.

Black and white. Smooth body. Sharp teeth.

Flags didn't have sharp teeth. This time it wasn't a mistake.

There was a killer whale swimming up and down the water-filled plane, blocking her way out.

Her friends had saved her from fighting an eel in a cave, then sent her off alone to face a killer whale on a plane.

Rona slumped her seal body into the pilot's chair, and tried to think.

She had at least ten minutes of oxygen left in her blood. Enough time to think for five minutes then swim for five. That would get her to the surface. But only if she could get past the whale.

She looked round the door. There was only one whale. Killer whales usually hunted in pods, in families of half a dozen or more. They didn't often hunt alone. However, one guardian was more appropriate for a quest. It gave the contestant a chance.

But not much of a chance. The killer whale was bigger, stronger and faster in a straight line than her. It couldn't manoeuvre as quickly, but in the empty plane, there was nothing for Rona to hide behind and not enough space for underwater gymnastics to confuse or evade the whale.

She peeked out again. It was patrolling the length of the plane, its body undulating up and down, a motion unlike any fish, a motion which sent terror along her spine. This was the monster from selkies' bedtime stories. Rona's worst nightmare.

When it turned at the end to come back, its body

nearly spanned the width of the plane, the largest cargo this plane had ever carried. Rona was almost hypnotised by the shimmering markings on its fat sleek body. Fat and sleek from eating seal meat.

As it swam towards Rona, it saw her and grinned, showing off its long sharp yellow teeth jutting up through its thick pink jaws. Seal-ripping teeth. Seal-crunching jaws.

She jerked back into the small metal room, and slammed the door shut. If this was a war plane, they must have had weapons. She frantically opened all the cupboards and the contents floated out: charts, a compass, hats, gloves. No human guns, selkie spears or blue-man knives.

The whole plane juddered. The whale was banging its head against the thin wall which separated them, trying to hurry her out, or to break in and drag her out.

Rona swam up to the ceiling then down to the floor. Surely the pilots had an emergency exit! Or their bodies would still be trapped here, wouldn't they?

Then, under the middle seat, she saw something bright red, something sharp.

An axe.

Rona brushed a starfish from its smooth surface. "For fire and emergency only" it said on the handle. Rona tugged it free with her fins.

There was another thump at the door. The whale was getting impatient for its breakfast.

Rona had to decide how she was leaving this plane. As a seal or a girl?

She was faster and more agile as a seal. But whales ate seals, and humans killed whales. A human with an axe might take the whale by surprise. And hands were more useful for tools.

She slipped out of her skin, shoved it into the satchel, and stretched her long human arms. She felt an immediate thirst for air. She would drown if she didn't turn back into a seal or get to the surface fast. But she had a killer whale to get past first. So she grasped the bright red axe.

She kicked open the door, hitting the whale on the nose. And swam out, whirling the axe in front of her.

The killer whale backed away, surprised. It had come to eat a nice juicy seal, and suddenly a human whacked it in the face and waved a metal weapon at it.

She swam at it again, but this time the whale didn't move back. It edged forward. So she slashed at its face with the axe.

The whale grinned its dolphin grin, ducked its head, clicked at her in clear submission and eased sideways out of her way.

That was easy, thought Rona, as she swam past the whale's harlequin body and towards the hole at the end of the plane.

Then she felt the water shift behind her as the whale spun round and lunged at her legs.

Rona somersaulted in the water, flipping herself up to the roof of the plane, and saw the treacherous whale swerve to follow her.

She aimed the axe and threw it two-handed with all her strength straight at the killer whale's mouth. She heard a thunk as the axe struck the whale's jaw, and saw one tooth spin out of its mouth. The whale hung in shock in the water, and Rona sprinted away.

As she dived out of the plane, a merman judge

nodded to her, and flapped a black and white flag at the entrance. Hoping that was a signal to the guardian that its job was done, Rona aimed for the brightness above.

She felt the lack of oxygen in her blood, lights were flickering at the edge of her vision, but she kept forcing herself up.

Finally she broke the surface, and breathed the sweet warm air.

She had to change into her seal self and swim back to the island. She circled round to find the southeast bearing which would get her home. She was putting her hand in the satchel to get out her skin, when she saw the surface of the water in front of her shiver and dimple.

She recognised that water pattern. It meant something was coming upwards through the sea so fast it was distorting the water above it.

Rona scooted sideways.

And the killer whale shot vertically out of the water.

Its sudden arrival showered her with spray; its open smiling mouth just missed her.

But it wouldn't miss again. This killer whale was determined to eat her. To throw her in the air, bat her with its tail and play with her like a toy, until it was bored and she was dead. Then it would eat her.

Here was her nightmare, splashing down into the water, just a few metres away.

Rona had her skin in her hand, but there was no point in changing. She couldn't outswim this predator. But she couldn't just give up. She hadn't finished the quest.

The whale spy-hopped, head out of the water, checking where she was, then dropped down and began to swim straight for her.

Rona shoved the skin back in the satchel, and wrapped her shaking hand round the pens rolling in the bottom of the wet bag, hoping they were all pointing the same way.

As the whale rocketed towards her on the surface, she raised her hand out of the water, a tight bundle of sharp pens poking out of her fist. Just before the whale reached her, she jinked to the side. The whale swung its head to follow her, and she jabbed at its eye with the nibs of all the pens.

Rona didn't hit the small dark target straight on, so the metal nibs scraped across the whale's eye, sliding off onto the thick rubbery skin.

But the killer whale squealed. An oddly high-pitched noise from such a large beast, like a child's whistle.

Rona hadn't succeeded in blinding the whale, but she had hurt it enough to distract it from the chase. It veered away from her, shrieking and slapping the water with its huge flat tail.

Rona didn't wait around to see if its family would answer its calls, nor if the judge would come up to see who'd survived the killer whale's rule-breaking.

She dived into her sealskin, turned her back on the moaning whale, and sprinted even faster than when she beat Tangaroa, towards the safety of her own island.

As she swam, Rona wondered if Yann had been right. Maybe they hadn't needed to cheat. Maybe she could have fought an eel on her own. Because eels couldn't be nearly as scary as killer whales ...

Chapter 27

Yann and his passengers arrived at Taltomie, and Helen ran into the tent to change out of the selkie dress and put on a pair of unchewed trainers. Then she rowed everyone over to Eilan nan MacCodrum to see who had won.

They found a tense group of families, friends and elders, with tattoos, fishtails and sealskin cloaks, waiting on the shore.

There was no sign of the contestants.

Helen started to worry. "Why isn't Rona back yet? Is the holder a long way away? Or is there more to the quest than just following the map to collect it ...?"

There was a shout from a selkie boy keeping a lookout on the highest point of the island, and the groups of supporters peered out to sea.

A sleek head rose from the water, an elegant shape swam through the waves, and everyone was silent as the first competitor back clambered onto the rocks.

Rona raised a green bottle high in the air, to delighted cheers from the selkies and polite applause from the blue men and mermaids.

Helen screamed in surprise, then hugged Yann, while Lavender and Catesby pirouetted in the air.

There was a flurry of foam as Tangaroa jumped out, waving another green bottle, then he saw Rona, and sank down in despairing exhaustion. Five minutes later, Serena swam up, but when she saw the others there already, she turned and swam off again, until her aunt fetched her back to congratulate Rona.

Helen sighed. "Rona won! The sea-through lost! She's the Sea Herald. It's all over."

But Lavender shook her head. "The bloom won't give up."

Yann agreed. "We have to assume the bloom will send the sea-through to attack Rona tomorrow as she delivers the message. And I don't know how we can protect her out there."

They all looked at the Atlantic Ocean, stretching to the horizon and beyond.

Selkies love holding feasts, Helen decided, as she munched another crunchy fishfinger. The crowd had been very enthusiastic when Helen and Rona performed together at the start of the feast, and now everyone was eating fancy seafood again. Rona was at the top table, looking tired, but also proud of the new chain of office round her neck.

The seating arrangements were similar to the Storm Singer feast, but this time the mermaids and blue loons were quiet and subdued. Serena and Tangaroa were both as exhausted as Rona, and neither of them had victory to give them energy. The feasting selkies were being a bit too loud and proud about their contestant's victory for the losers to relax and enjoy the food.

The only selkie who didn't look pleased was Sinclair. He'd snapped at Roxburgh so loudly for spilling a jug of water that everyone looked round, and Roxburgh turned bright red and sank lower in his seat. Helen noticed Roxburgh didn't eat or drink anything else until his dad went to the top table to speak to Strathy, and to pat Rona on the shoulder with a stretched smile on his face.

"The sea-through's team are all looking pretty wretched," said Yann. "Maybe the bloom doesn't have a plan for tomorrow after all."

After the third fish course, Rona came down to their table. "I'm falling asleep in this warm cave. Let's go and breathe some sea air."

So they rowed out to the beach, where Yann insisted on showing them the deep marks made by the blue loons as he pulled them along the beach during the tug-of-war. As Yann was pacing out his triumph for the girls, a familiar voice said, "Yes. We've all been well beaten this week."

Yann galloped up to stand protectively over Rona, but Tangaroa just sat down beside her. "I wanted to say well done, without all the fancy words my elders expect me to use. Anyone who can answer riddles that fast, swim that far, and overcome all their obvious fears to pass two guardians, deserves to be Sea Herald. Good for you, Rona."

Helen looked at him in the warm glow of Lavender's lightballs. He didn't seem angry, just tired.

"What about finding your way home?" she asked. "Aren't you upset about losing your chance to ask the powers where you're from?"

"I have at least three other ideas for finding the right island, none of which involve rhymes or tattoos, so I'll just keep trying." He shrugged and smiled at Rona. "So what did you fight then?"

Rona bit her lip, and Helen had a horrible feeling she was about to confess, so Helen said firmly, "There was a giant eel in a cave and a killer whale on a plane. You?"

"A kelpie and a killer whale."

There was a laugh from out at sea, and Serena appeared from the black waves. "Me too. A giant squid and ANOTHER killer whale. Not very ORIGINAL." She joined them on the sand.

"Anyone get bitten?" asked Tangaroa.

Rona said, "Helen did. On the ankle."

There was a moment of silence.

Helen laughed. "Yes! I did get bitten. By midgies! It was far more dangerous watching the quest than facing all those monsters." She scratched the graze on her ankle.

Tangaroa laughed too, but Serena sighed. "Ankles ... I did hope for properly working ankles at last. But I didn't win ANYTHING. Not one task. I was a complete failure."

"No, you weren't," said Tangaroa. "You *finished* every

task. We all did. That hardly ever happens. So any of us is qualified to be a Sea Herald. It's just Rona was the best. Why did you think you'd get working ankles by winning?"

"I planned to ask the sea powers about the witch who cursed us to walk on fire, so I can persuade her to lift the curse."

"Just like me," Tangaroa said sympathetically. "I hoped to ask for the way home. What will you do now?"

"I'll stop looking for shortcuts and do some proper research. There MUST be others who know where that witch is." Serena flicked her hair back. "Anyway, if I'm stuck with this tail for now, can the human healer overcome her midgie bites, and put more sealant on?"

Helen nodded, and went back to the boat for the spare bicycle repair kit she'd hidden there. As she walked through the dark, she wondered about Tangaroa and Serena's answers.

When she got back, she asked for brighter lightballs and looked at the sealant on Serena's tail. It was thinning at the edges, but it had worked. She peeled off the original layer, apologising as Serena moaned theatrically.

"Do you really want me to paint another layer on, Serena? The contest is over. You could let your tail heal out of the water."

"It's traditional for the sea tribes to accompany a new Sea Herald for the first mile," said Serena. "I want to swim with Rona tomorrow. Otherwise I'd look like a bad loser. And I'm NOT a bad loser, really I'm not."

Helen made a decision. As she applied the glue, she asked, "Would you have cheated to get uncursed legs, or the way home?"

"Helen!" said Lavender, but Helen ignored her.

Serena said, through gritted teeth, "You don't know much about curses, human. If you lift a curse by cheating, you bring a WORSE curse down on yourself. I wouldn't have cheated to win, because it wouldn't have worked."

"Me neither," said Tangaroa. "The way home might not be found by rhyme, but it certainly won't be found by dishonesty. What kind of home-coming would that be?"

Helen persisted, "So if some creature had offered to stop Rona winning and help you win, what would you have said?"

"Don't be DAFT," said Serena. "The judges would have noticed any outside help."

"Not if it was transparent," said Tangaroa slowly. "You accused me on the first day, Rona, of working with a sea-through. Did it attack you again? Did it try to help me or Serena again?"

"Yes," said Rona, "it held up two of my canoes in the second task."

"I wondered why those orange ones kept bobbing back up," said Serena.

"And on the quest," Yann said carefully, "once the map guardian was defeated, the sea-through tried to steal the map."

"So you won DESPITE the sea-through trying to stop you in each task?" asked Serena.

"And you thought we were behind it?" Tangaroa said angrily. "How dare you?"

"How DARE the sea-through interfere!" spat Serena. "Even if I had won, I could NEVER have lifted the curse with a tainted win behind me. The sea-through was ruining it for ALL of us!"

"And ruining my reputation," muttered Tangaroa, "if anyone thinks I would work with a lump of jelly to win a race or a fight. I would rather be beaten fair and square than win by cheating. Yann," he looked up, "you understand, don't you?"

"Oh yes," Yann said quietly. "I understand."

"So you're both angry with the sea-through for interfering with the contest?" Helen asked.

They nodded.

Helen lowered her voice. "We don't think it's stopped interfering yet, and we know it's in league with at least one selkie elder, so if we tell you what it wants, will you keep it quiet for now?"

Tangaroa and Serena agreed, so Helen explained what they'd discovered about the bloom's plans, finishing by saying, "We think the bloom will send the sea-through to attack Rona again tomorrow, because it wants to change the message and provoke real war, so the coast will be destroyed and the sea will get back all that it once owned."

"But all the humans, all the boats ... That would be AWFUL!" gasped Serena.

"It would be a disaster for the sea tribes too," said Tangaroa, "because most sea people live on the edge between land and sea. What can we do to stop the bloom succeeding?"

"You both completed the tasks, you're both qualified to be Sea Heralds," said Helen. "Could you accompany Rona not just for the first mile, but the whole way? Guard her and the message, so the sea-through can't prevent her getting through?"

Tangaroa grinned. "I'd love to."

Serena looked down at her tail. "I'd be happy to. Do you think I'll need an extra layer of sealant?"

But Yann kicked the sand and whispered, "Helen, Rona, Lavender, Catesby, could I have a word?" He led them further up the beach. "Helen, this is foolish. How do we know they're not working with the sea-through? How do we know they're telling the truth?"

Lavender said, "Serena's right, some curses can detect trickery. I'm less sure about Tangaroa, because blue men are happy to drown people to get rhymes, and cheating to find the way home isn't as bad as murder."

Yann shrugged. "It depends on your code of honour. He might be telling the truth. But only *might be*."

Helen smiled. "You don't want to believe them, because if they're telling the truth, then we didn't need to cheat. Let's worry about our own honesty later, and think about Rona's safety right now. What do you think, Sea Herald?"

"We have to trust them," said Rona. "The three coastal tribes should work together tomorrow to save the coast." She turned back towards the blue loon and the mermaid.

As they walked to the water's edge, Helen asked Rona, "Do you have to collect the message from Thalas *before* you swim to Merras at dawn tomorrow? You must get up really early."

"Normally the herald does visit the challenger first, but someone reminded Strathy that traditionally one of the elders collects the message on the night of the contest because the new Sea Herald is tired after all the tasks. I'll be given it, in the herald's holder, tomorrow morning."

Rona yawned, which set off a chorus of yawns from everyone: girl, fairy, mermaid, blue loon, phoenix and centaur. They all laughed, then arranged to meet in the morning at Skerness.

Tangaroa held out his hand to Rona. "I will use all my strength and speed to make sure you and the message get through."

Serena held out her hand too. "It will be a PRIVILEGE to swim with you both."

Yann said in an undertone, "I hope we've chosen our allies well."

Lavender whispered, "We won't know, until they all come back."

Chapter 28

Next morning, it was impossible for Helen to speak to Rona at the wide beach by Skerness Point. The new Sea Herald was surrounded by well-wishers, with speeches, songs, and help fitting the bottle into the chain round her neck.

As Tangaroa and Serena were taking their responsibilities seriously and staying close to Rona, Helen couldn't speak to them either.

So she settled on a rock with her fiddle, and played along with the celebratory music.

When the sun rose, Rona's four land-bound friends watched her dive into the water, then a cheering group of selkies, mermaids and blue men followed her out of the bay.

Helen packed her violin away, and looked round. Past Yann's broad back, the beach was empty.

Except for one sad shape, hunched on the sand to their right.

She recognised the pattern of blotches on the seal's back. "Is that Roxburgh? Why hasn't he gone with everyone else?"

"Probably sulking," said Yann. "Just leave him alone."

"Let's try to cheer him up. It's not his fault he's a good singer or his dad's a traitor. He didn't ask to be the sea-through's puppet."

She walked across the sand to the depressed-looking seal, who took one look at her with his huge sad eyes, and slid into the water.

Catesby laughed, and Yann said, "Well done, Helen. That really cheered him up."

Helen watched as Roxburgh surfaced out at sea, his dark head bobbing up and down, staring at them. She shouted, "Rona will be fine, the other Sea Herald contestants will look after her."

"Shh!" said Yann. "Don't tell the whole ocean our cunning plan!"

"He looks worried, I'm just trying to ..."

The seal's head vanished.

"Great," said Yann. "If he's off to tell the bloom she's got a guard, it might send more than its usual single sea-through!"

Then Roxburgh's human form stepped onto the beach, and walked towards them.

"It's all over," he said in his most tragic, sobbing, musical voice. "The coast will be destroyed, the sea will own everything and my father will be king of a wet wasteland. I hadn't realised! I don't want to be prince of death and destruction."

"It's fine," said Helen. "The other tribes are protecting her, the message will get though."

"The message will get through!" Roxburgh laughed. "So it will. But that will make things worse!" He walked off, hunched and miserable, as the friends shrugged at each other.

Then Helen saw his shoulders straighten. He turned and ran back to them. "You can sort it out! You have land magic and power, and the sea-through has never quite beaten you. I can't do anything, but you can sort it out."

"Sort what out?" asked Lavender.

"The message. My father switched the message. He reminded Strathy last night of the tradition that a first-time Sea Herald is given a night off, that an elder fetches the message from the challenging power. And Strathy let my *father* get it from Thalas. So father made a new deal with the sea-through. The sea-through wrote a different message, put it in one of the losers' holders, and gave it to my father. That's the message efficient little Rona and her friends are delivering. Not a ritual challenge. An insult.

"It goes something like this:

"To Merras the withered. I am tired of pretending to fight on equal terms with you, when I see your muscles grow weak, your fish grow grey, your currents sink low and your power ebb away. It is my duty to use my superior strength to crush your pathetic body under my sandy feet, to rule the waters all year round, and to seize back what belongs to the sea. Prepare for defeat. From Thalas the conqueror."

"That will definitely provoke war!" gasped Yann.

"Can you stop it?" Roxburgh looked at them hopefully.

Helen said, "What exactly do you think we can *do*, Roxburgh? We can't swim after Rona. We can't go to the powers and explain. We're land people."

"Where is the original message?" asked Lavender. "Could we still get it to Merras? Your dad must have collected it from Thalas, or Thalas would be suspicious. Is it with your family's possessions on the island?"

"No," moaned Roxburgh. "He swapped bottles with the sea-through. The true message is in the middle of the bloom."

"Could we write our own message?" suggested Yann. "Write a politer message from Thalas to Merras, or even an explanation?"

"That wouldn't work. It has to be in a proper herald's holder." Roxburgh shook his head. "No, not even you can help. It's impossible!"

"Don't give up yet," said Helen. "Let's climb the headland, and see if the bloom is still where Lavender and Catesby saw it."

Yann led the way off the beach and up the slope to the headland, where Helen stood on the very edge of the cliff and looked out to sea. When she wrinkled her eyes, there was a faint pink sheen on the surface of the sea. "Is that it?"

Lavender nodded. "Yes, that's close to where we heard it chant."

"I could row out there," said Helen doubtfully, "but I don't know what I'd do when I got there."

They heard a massive roar. They saw a ripple start on the horizon. A high wave rushed towards the shore, crashing into the feet of the two stacks at the point of the headland.

Then there was silence.

"Merras has read the insult," wailed Roxburgh. "It's too late ... she's going to attack Thalas."

"It's never too late," said Yann firmly. "If we deliver the true message to her in the herald's holder, she might stop."

"But the message and holder are out at sea," Helen pointed out. "And the sea is about to turn into a battleground! We can't go and get the message."

Another roar rolled from the sea, like wet echoing thunder, and Helen almost turned and ran towards Ben Loyal and its reassuring height, or the moors far inland ...

But then she looked at the bloom again, rocking gently on the water after the first waves of anger had passed.

"We can't go to the bloom," she said suddenly, "but it can come to us."

"Don't be daft," said Yann. "Why would it come inshore? It can ride out the battle storm in the deep water, but it would be smashed to pieces on the shore."

Helen grinned. "In the olden days, wreckers attracted ships onto the rocky parts of this coast with lights, watched as they broke on the rocks, then collected all the valuable cargo. We could smash the bloom on the rocks at the base of the cliff, then clamber down and find the message."

"How will we get it to come shorewards? Wave a lantern?"

Helen gestured to the rising mountains of water already building up over the battling sea powers. "We'll sing up a storm and pull the bloom inland."

"But we don't have a Storm Singer!"

"Yes, we do. Roxburgh is almost as good a singer as Rona. He could have won all on his own, if she hadn't had the technique I suggested. Roxburgh can sing up a storm."

"No, I can't!" Roxburgh backed away. "I can't even make up my own songs without father coaching me."

"I'm sure you can. Anyway, you don't have to sing a storm up from scratch. There's enough moving water out there for any number of storms. All you have to do is direct it, use it as a weapon to drag the bloom between the stacks and onto the rocks."

"I can't!"

"Yes, you can," said Yann, standing tall behind him. "Unless you want to be prince of nothing but a watery graveyard."

Roxburgh looked up at the frowning centaur above him, then out at the turmoil on the horizon. "What do I have to do?"

"Sing the song you and Rona sang at the competition," explained Helen, "but don't stick to the simple rhythm you learnt as a pup. Listen to the water. Hear the pauses, the moments when the water is hanging and waiting, and sing into those, persuade the water to join you. Speed up with the water as it rushes to shore, and breathe the wind movements as you breathe in and out. Listen to it, use it as backing, then draw it into your song."

"Is that what Rona did?"

"Sort of, though she had to pull a storm from calm weather. You already have a storm. You can do it."

So Roxburgh started to sing.

At his first attempt, his voice cracked. He had to sing the first line three times before he made it to the second line. Helen nodded encouragingly.

But once he got going, he sang the song exactly like he'd sung it at the competition.

Helen grunted in frustration. "No! Listen to the wind and waves. Hear them and sing into them."

He started again. This time he kept stopping to listen, then losing the thread of the melody.

Helen shook her head, and swung her fiddle off her back. "Like this." She played the melody, like she had on the beach rehearsing with Rona just three days ago.

As she played she joined the beat of the storm, and tapped her feet and chanted the words, to emphasize and encourage the crashing waves and howling wind, so the storm sounded closer and the music sounded like part of the storm.

She stopped. Roxburgh was staring at her. "You're doing it, human girl! You just keep doing it."

"No, I'm not a selkie, I don't have magic. I can't call the storm. But I can keep the music going, if you sing."

Helen started to play again, and Roxburgh, more confident now he had someone to follow, added his powerful voice to Helen's rhythm.

Helen felt the storm move closer. Her hair whipped about, her eyes stung with spray, and she barely noticed when Lavender hid in her fleece, while Yann held Catesby to his chest. The centaur stood to the seaward side of the fiddler and singer, to shield them from the rising weather.

The storm moved closer. The waves moved closer.

"Maybe it's not us," gasped Helen, "maybe they're just starting to fight closer."

"No," yelled Yann. "It *is* you, you're pulling it right towards us."

Helen peered over his back and saw the bloom writhing in the water, a pink mass struggling to get free of the white waves throwing it towards the coast. She could see the vast baggy stomach and the wriggling edge of thousands of tangled tentacles, caught in the surge of water towards the shore.

Helen called to Roxburgh, "Change song! We need something louder, harsher, to get it on the rocks, not the beach." Roxburgh nodded and started to sing about a storm bubbling up from the sea.

Helen needed a moment to get the notes right, so he stopped singing, unsure what to do without her accompaniment.

"Keep going!" yelled Yann. "The bloom is sliding out of the storm's fingers!"

Helen and Roxburgh started up again, louder, faster, more confident, though they were being lashed by wind and spray.

Now he'd grasped the idea, Roxburgh was giving it everything: huge volume, huge emotion, and singing like the world was listening poised to applaud. Finally, he had the confidence to add his own notes to the tune, and that was when the storm really started to batter the coast.

"It's too near," warned Yann. "We have to move back."

"No," shouted Helen, "we have to stay here, we have to hear the sea, or we can't sing the storm. You can move back through."

But Yann dug his hooves into the turf and shielded them, as the storm, the waves and the bloom got closer.

Helen watched the bloom being thrown towards them, looking like a heap of soggy old pink party balloons trailing poisonous ribbons.

The waves rose higher, so it wasn't just spray and wind hitting them now. Solid sheets of water were falling on their heads. Helen hunched over, trying to protect her violin.

Below them, the two stacks, the Old Man and Old Woman of Skerness, were channelling the waters, breaking the waves into a chaos of white and grey, then pink and purple. Sea-throughs were being ripped off the tattered edges of the bloom.

The bloom was being lifted so far up by the waves that at the highest point, when Roxburgh reached the highest notes, the bloom was opposite them, hundreds of sea-through eyes staring at them in shock and hatred. Then the wave crashed down again and the bloom was dragged away.

Helen had an idea, and started to play high and low notes in a relentless rhythm. Roxburgh copied her and between them they raised the incoming waves even higher and the crashing falls even lower.

Helen yelled, "Stop, on four!"

As they played the next high notes, the bloom was lifted so far into the air that they could see underneath it to all its dangling tentacles.

Then Helen and Roxburgh stopped, suddenly, on the same beat.

The wave fell.

And the bloom fell.

Right onto the stacks. Right onto the Old Man and Old Woman of Skerness.

The stacks stabbed through the centre of the bloom like two spears, and the bloom disintegrated.

All the sea-throughs let go, and slid down the stacks,

or landed in jellied heaps on the headland, or crashed down onto the rocks, or clutched the cliff edge and pulled themselves up, struggling to change into their landforms as they slithered around.

The western stack, the Old Man, split in two, and crumbled into the sea.

Catesby squawked, pulled himself free from Yann's protective arms, and flew straight into the wind.

The phoenix soared over the stacks, dodging falling jellyfish, and seized the green bottle, which had been thrown up and out of the ripped bloom.

But as the phoenix struggled to stay airborne with the weight of the bottle in his claws, a transparent hand snatched him out of the air.

The tall sea-through stood near the edge of the cliff, surrounded by creeping and scuttling sea-throughs. Helen saw it was twice the size of the others from the bloom, which were sliding off the cliff, escaping into the water below.

Catesby held the bottle, and the sea-through held Catesby.

"The message is written in squid ink on fishskin," hissed the sea-through. "And the bottle came from a wreck. The sea wants them back. They will come with me, back to the sea. And the bird in my hand comes too."

Catesby pecked and struggled, but couldn't get free of the long stretchy fingers.

The sea-through laughed, and took one step back. Yann stepped forward. "The bird doesn't belong to the sea."

"It does now!" giggled the sea-through and took another step.

Then Helen saw a wave rise silently out of the sea behind the cliff. Not a long line of surf, but a narrow finger of water.

The wave wrapped itself round the sea-through's neck, lifted it high into the air, and as fast as Helen had ever seen water move, slapped the sea-through down onto the edge of the cliff, like a bird smashing a shell on a rock. The sea-through flung open its hands in shock, dropping the phoenix and the bottle.

The wave pulled the squealing sea-through down to the sea.

Immediately Yann ran forward to lift the gasping Catesby, and Helen grabbed the bottle before it rolled over the edge.

They saw the narrow white wave drag the sea-through between the stacks, the tall Old Woman and the stump of the Old Man, and down deep into the sea.

They looked at the smaller sea-throughs, sliding off the rocks, bobbing in the waves. Not joining up again, swimming off separately.

"We had stopped playing," Helen said slowly. "We didn't sing up that wave. That wasn't part of the storm."

Roxburgh croaked, "No, that was the sea."

"It was all the sea," said Helen.

Lavender spoke from inside Helen's collar, "He's right. That was the sea. Doing what the sea-through always said the sea would do. Taking its own. But only its own. The sea has left us everything else, everything we need to stop the battle."

Helen nodded. "If we're going to stop the battle, we have to get the true message to Merras. Roxburgh, you'll have to swim with it ..." She turned to give the bottle to the selkie. But all she saw was a sobbing heap of sealskin on the ground.

Yann shook his head. "He would never have made a Sea Herald. He doesn't have the stamina."

"So who's going to take it?" asked Helen.

Catseby, Lavender and Yann looked at her.

She sighed. "Alright. Let's get the boat."

As Helen slid off Yann's back near the campsite, the centaur said, "We'll all come."

"No. And no arguments. I have to go alone. The boat is faster without you. You go inland. Save yourselves. If I don't succeed, find some elders the sea powers will listen to, and get the truth to Merras and Thalas somehow, before the battle destroys the whole coast. But save yourselves first."

She didn't wait for goodbyes, she just clambered over the wall, and ran through the campsite.

The Scouts looked at her strangely as they slotted bikes into racks on the minibuses.

"You're having an early start," said Emily. "It looks nasty, you shouldn't go out to sea."

"I probably shouldn't," Helen agreed. "Where are you going?"

"We're cycling up round the clearance village."

"Excellent," said Helen. "The views are best from really far inland. Get going now, before the weather gets worse."

She ran for the boat, leapt in, wedged the bottle between her feet and grabbed the oars.

Helen looked back at the coast as she rowed out to sea, wondering if the campsite would still be there tomorrow, wondering if she'd ever see her friends again.

Chapter 29

Taltomie Bay was calm, sheltered from the storm by the island, so Helen rowed across easily. When she turned round, she could see a whirl of water and air on the horizon, and a sparkle of lightning in the sky. She and Roxburgh had only summoned the very edge of that storm to destroy the bloom. Most of it was still out there, still raging.

Could she row through that? Should she?

If she got through it, what would she find? What were the sea powers like? How could she tell which was Merras and which was Thalas? And was there any point in a human girl yelling, "There's been a misunderstanding. Please stop trying to kill each other so you can read this tiny little message in this teeny little bottle"?

But they must be used to getting messages in bottles, even if they weren't used to human messengers, so she kept rowing steadily.

Once she was past the selkies' island, the waves and wind got stronger, and the boat was harder to control. But Helen just kept rowing, the bottle between her feet, and the rhythm of the sea in her mind.

Then she hit something.

She stopped rowing and jerked round. The bow wasn't holed; the boat wasn't sinking. What had she hit?

She noticed something floating by her left oar, groaning, and Helen reached into the churning sea and dragged out ... Rona, who slipped off her sealskin and rubbed her forehead.

"Helen! What are you doing here? We have to get home! The message made Merras really angry and now they're fighting. Turn round, row back!"

"Where are Serena and Tangaroa?"

"I don't know. When Merras read the message, she started to stamp on the seabed and slap the surface. The waves ripped us apart, and I haven't seen Tangaroa or Serena since. I have to get back and tell the elders something has gone wrong, so Strathy can work out what to do."

"I know what's wrong. You delivered the wrong message. Sinclair switched it last night. You delivered a terrible insult from Thalas to Merras, so they're starting a real fight. But we've already retrieved the original message from the bloom. If we can get this true message to Merras, perhaps they'll stop fighting before the battle reaches the coastline."

Rona sighed in exhaustion. "Give it to me. I'll swim back."

"No, we should go together: one of us to hand over the real message, and the other to explain to Thalas why Merras is so angry. They can't make peace unless they both realise what went wrong."

So Rona shouted directions to avoid the worst of the unpredictable waves, and Helen rowed harder than ever to get into the heart of the storm.

As they got nearer, the boat seemed too small and light to withstand the beating of the water, but also too large and heavy for Helen to force it through the thrashing sea. And the cold white teeth on the edge of every wave bit down towards the girls.

But Helen kept driving the boat forward, away from the land, into the deep and deeper sea. The storm howled above their heads, ripping off the tops of waves, and mixing the sea with the wind. There was so much water in the air that Helen could hardly breathe, so much air in the water that the oars had almost nothing to push against.

Helen yelled, "I can't row against these waves any more. Rona, can you calm the waters down a bit?"

"How?"

"You can sing them up, surely you can sing them down again. Try a lullaby ..."

Rona started singing softly and Helen twisted round and watched the waves in front of the boat flatten. The surprised selkie smoothed a path for Helen to row towards the two battling powers. The boat sped forward through a tunnel of flat water with the spray and chaos of the storm arching over it.

Then Rona yelled, "Look round. Can you see them?"

Helen peered through the walls of spray, and saw two massive shapes, outlined by lightning against the dark clouds. A man and woman so tall they were standing only ankle-deep in the ocean. Merras and Thalas.

They were made of swirling water. Huge and hypnotic, beautiful and terrifying, just like the ocean. They had armour made of shoals of fish swimming just below the surface of their thin watery skin, and green arms with waves racing along them as they flexed their muscles. They had faces of foam, and hair of windblown sand.

That was how Helen could tell them apart. One had hair made of spiky black volcanic sand. He must be Thalas. The other had hair flowing to her waist, of golden sand like the long beaches of the Western Isles. She must be Merras.

They were screaming and throwing spears of broken masts and lumps of ripped up seabed at each other.

Helen shouted, "Why are they fighting up here if they're deep sea powers?"

Rona yelled back, "How well they keep their shape in the air shows off their strength. Are you sure you want to get closer?"

Helen turned her back on them, and kept rowing, as Rona wore her voice out singing a safe path through the battle storm.

Finally they were right between the two fighting giants, hoping neither would drop their weapons onto the tiny boat below.

Helen picked up the bottle, and shouted, "I'll get this to Merras, because the message should speak for itself. You talk to Thalas, because we don't have anything to show him and he's more likely to listen to a selkie than a human."

"If he can hear anything," screamed Rona over the roaring above and around them.

"But how do we get their attention? We're down at their ankles!"

"I've done that already today. You dive into them."

"Dive *into* them?"

"They're made of sea and currents and tides. Just dive into them and you'll be able to swim higher to where they can see and hear you. Watch me."

Rona slid out of the boat, still in human form, swam swiftly to Thalas's ankle, and with her hands together as if she was going to dive off a board, sliced through the surface of his skin and swam into his leg.

Helen watched, amazed, as a current drew Rona up his leg, towards his torso.

Taking a deep breath, she grasped the bottle, jumped out of the boat, and swam towards Merras's right leg.

She snatched one more breath as she reached the pillar of water, linked her hands round the bottle, and dived forwards.

She was immediately grabbed by a warm tight grip, like a hug from someone much bigger, and thrust up the pillar. She could see that Rona was still moving through Thalas. Helen held her breath, held the bottle and let the water tow her along.

Suddenly she was in a much wider space, Merras's belly, still moving upwards, then she was caught in a chaos of currents, which battered and confused her. Helen guessed she was in Merras's heart, where all the currents met, so she kicked off towards an outstretched arm, and felt another current drag her along.

When she could see the water splitting into five paths ahead of her, she surged through the surface of the water, pushed out into the air, gulped a breath, and stood on the palm of a huge woman made of moving water.

Helen looked up at the enormous, scowling face of Merras, with her glowing green eyes and coral white teeth. The deep sea power roared, louder than the storm, "Why do you disturb me in my fight against that insulting upstart?"

Helen looked round. Rona was shivering on Thalas's palm, waving her hands, pointing to Helen. So Helen held up the bottle to Merras. "This is the true Sea Herald message. This morning's message was a forgery, sent by the sea-through bloom, not Thalas. We're delivering the true message to you, and an explanation to him."

She offered the bottle to Merras, who picked it out of her hand and crushed it between her thumb and finger. As sharp fragments fell to the sea below, she peered at the message.

She spoke, in a softer, less angry voice: "This is more complimentary. He's noticed my new hairstyle. This is in the usual words, from one equal to another. This is not an insult. This is the true message?"

Helen nodded.

"The insult this morning was from a cnidaree bloom?"

Helen nodded again.

"Your selkie companion is explaining this to Thalas?"

Helen nodded a third time.

Merras roared again. But this time it was a laugh.

"Hey, Thalas!" she shouted. "Thanks for noticing my hair."

He boomed back, "Thanks for a great fight!"

"It is good to know we both still have the strength to fight a true fight."

"Yes, but we don't need to prove it again for many years!"

"Your turn to rule for six months, then," said Merras. "I'll send a politer message with the herald when I challenge you in the spring."

Thalas said, "Peace, friend?"

Merras answered, "Shake on it."

As the deep sea powers reached out their hands, with Helen and Rona still on their palms, Helen realised that the gesture of peace was going to crush them. So Helen reached out towards Rona, and as soon as the girls' hands met in the air, they grasped each other and jumped, while above them Thalas and Merras smashed their palms together, and laughed loudly, creating one last pattern of waves rushing to shore.

Helen and Rona fell down into the deep dark cold sea, filled with dead fish and sediment. Helen swallowed water as she hit and started to sink, eyes fogged and brain too overloaded to work out which way was up.

Rona wrapped her arms round Helen, pulled her to the surface and shoved her into the boat.

"Come on," she said, "let's go home."

Rona and Helen took one oar each, their faces to the two powers, who were sinking slowly into the sea, voices whispering together, "Now where are those sea-throughs? We shall send those little pink squidges to every corner of the ocean. They will never join up in our waters again."

The girls rowed quietly southwards.

There was no need to sing a calm path because the sea was rocking like a cradle, pushing them gently home to shore.

Chapter 30

Another selkie feast, thought Helen. They never just ate fish and chips on their laps. It was always something fancy.

But she didn't complain. She had Yann, his hair and tail brushed to Lavender's satisfaction, kneeling at one side of her; Serena and Tangaroa, both covered in bruises after being thrown on the rocks by the sea battle, sitting on the other; and Lavender and Catesby perched on the table in front.

Helen was watching Rona telling the gathering about the bloom's plot, Sinclair's bargain, and the journey through the storm to deliver the real message. Rona told the whole story, except the details of how she'd won the third task. When she finished, two selkie elders with stern faces marched a protesting Sinclair to an inner cave.

Then Rona reminded the gathering that Roxburgh had exposed his father's plot and helped defeat the bloom, so Roxburgh found himself cheered as loudly as his father had been booed.

Yann whispered, "Those cheers should be for you, Helen. You brought the storm to shore just as much as he did."

Helen just smiled, and waited for Rona to finish her speech so she could join them for more sponge fingers. But Rona wasn't finished yet.

"I am honoured to be your Sea Herald, but I did not win the honour in an honest contest. The sea-through interfered too much with the tasks for any result to be legitimate. I am content with being a Storm Singer. So I resign as Sea Herald."

There were gasps all round the cave. But Rona still hadn't finished.

"A new Sea Herald will have to be chosen next spring. I hope the losing contestants from this autumn equinox, who proved themselves worthy heralds today, will get another chance to compete. And I believe our other true Storm Singer, Roxburgh, should be the selkie contestant."

Everyone but Tangaroa and Serena cheered. They both sighed.

"It's very honourable of her to resign," said Tangaroa, "though I don't know if I can do all that again."

Serena nodded. "We'll CERTAINLY need six months to recover first!"

But Roxburgh was puffing out his chest and nodding to his friends.

Rona finally sat down, and Strathy stood up. "If you

must resign, then we will hold the contest again at the spring equinox. But there is one other person who has a right to compete, someone who has been both Storm Singer and Sea Herald today.

"Human bard, Helen Strang, do you wish to compete for the honour of being our Sea Herald?"

Helen glanced round. Yann nodded enthusiastically. Lavender shook her head. Serena shrugged. Tangaroa grinned. And Catesby chattered some wise advice. Which Helen didn't understand.

She smiled at the selkie top table. "Thank you very much, but no. I think I'll stay on dry land for a while. All this seawater isn't good for my fiddle."

Helen sat back comfortably, surrounded by her friends, old and new, and started to wipe the salt off her violin.

"Yann," she asked quietly, "can you describe what the sea powers' hair looks like? Or their armour?"

Yann scowled at her.

"Yann? Do I know something you don't know? Am I one step ahead of you?"

"Not really, human girl. I'm a whole six months ahead of you. Because I know ..."

"What? What do you know?"

He lowered his voice. "I know who will win the next Sea Herald contest."

"Who?" Helen demanded.

Yann grinned. "That's a riddle you'll have to work out for yourself ..."

Read on for a sneak preview
of the fourth and final
Fabled Beast Chronicles series

Maze Running
and
Other Magical Missions

Helen was crouched down, leaning into the hedge, listening. Hoping for a clip clop. Or a scrape. Or a yell for help. Anything that would prove Yann was alive.

But all she heard was the Master's rasping voice start the next verse in the song of sacrifice.

She glanced up. Lavender was just above her head, looking panicky. Catesby was shifting nervously in the tree. Sapphire was circling lower.

Suddenly Helen heard: *clip clop clip CRASH!*

Then a throaty growl, several splintering thuds, fast hoofbeats and a deep voice yelling, "Stop him!"

Helen stood up.

Yann galloped round the corner, a skinny silvery shape held to his chest. "Your turn now, human girl. Take her and get out. I'll hold them off..."

He shoved the pale baby into her arms, grinned at her, then swung round, pulling his bow and arrows off his back.

Helen clutched the long legs and light body of the baby, and tried not to let the baby's sharp spiral horn jab her shoulder as she ran through the maze.

The scorched smell from the baby's burnt mane was choking her, but she tried not to cough, so she could hear Lavender's instructions. "Turn left. Follow the tunnel. Keep running. You're nearly at a junction. Turn right, right again. You're nearly there!"

And Helen could see the back gate. A cheat's way out if you were playing a game; an essential get-away if you were being chased.

Rona yanked the gate open. Helen ran through. Rona slammed it and locked it. Then the selkie said softly, "Is she ok?"

Helen looked down. The fabled beast in her arms was singed and shivering. But the baby unicorn was still alive, which was all that mattered.

That, and getting all of her friends safely away from the maze.

So where was Yann?

Rona examined the base of the unicorn's slim horn. "We got here just in time. They hadn't started sawing it off. A unicorn this young couldn't have survived the shock of losing her horn."

Helen was relieved she wouldn't need the first aid kit on her back to heal any sacrificial wounds. She hugged the baby unicorn and smiled. She'd never been this close to a unicorn before; they were really shy, even of other fabled beasts. The panicked unicorn filly who had staggered into their midst this morning hadn't been able to look any of them in the eye, even when she was begging for their help.

But the baby in Helen's arms looked up at her with big golden eyes. Then Helen saw a blur of purple silk and feathers hover in front of her. "Stop gazing at the pretty pony," said Lavender, "we have to get away."

Catesby reinforced the point with a flick of his new copper feathers.

"We can't go without Yann," said Helen.

"We have to get the baby away first," insisted Rona, "because she's in the greatest danger. Yann will catch up with us."

Sapphire flapped above them, her blue wings blocking the dawn sky. But as Helen and the others stepped away from the maze into the rough ground where the dragon was going to land, Catesby squawked a warning.

Helen couldn't identify any words in the phoenix's croaking call. She couldn't understand Sapphire either. Even after more than a year, Helen couldn't understand any fabled beasts who didn't speak with a human voice. But it was clear from Catesby's jabbing beak that he was worried about the corner of the maze to her right.

Helen looked over and saw a herd of dirty white goats trotting round the sharp green corner.

Like the fauns the Master usually surrounded himself with, these goats were running on two legs, but unlike the fauns, they didn't have human torsos and heads. They were goat all the way up.

Helen didn't hang about to play spot the difference, she just assumed they weren't friendly and turned to run round the maze in the other direction.

But as she skidded round the corner and sprinted down a lawn bounded by the maze on one side and a straight line of trees on the other, she saw goat creatures coming from the ancient stone house at the front of the maze too.

Helen and her friends were caught in a pincer movement.

She yelled upwards, "Sapphire, there's no time for us to climb on your back before they reach us. We'll meet you on the other side of these trees."

Then Helen ran away from the maze, shouting behind her, "Yann! Get out of there! We're under attack!"

To be continued ...